Desert Falcon

Leslie Goodyear

&

Fergus Beley

Copyright

Desert Falcon – A Legend

Copyright © 2018, by Leslie Goodyear & Fergus Beeley

All rights reserved. Thank you for purchasing an authorized edition of this book and for complying with copyright laws by not reproducing, scanning or distributing any part of this book in any form without permission. Ebooks are not transferrable. To contact the publisher for permissions, please write to desertfalcon@freestonepublishing.com

This book is a work of fiction. The names, characters, places and incidents are products of the writers' imagination or have been used factiously and are not to be construed as real. Any resemblance to persons, living or dead, actual events, locale or organizations is entirely coincidental

ISBN: 978-0-692-066539 Paperback
ISBN: 978-0-692-06927 Ebook

Design by Freestone Publishing
Cover photo "Bedouin Girl" by Fergus Beeley

For Sheikha

1.

Wise and wrathful as a grandmother, the desert shifts like the ocean, tied to the mark of time itself, and keeps its stories as it pleases. As giant muses, her dunes walk like liquid through generations, whispering in voices heard by those born of her, by those still enough to hear, and by those whom they choose. Literatures of families rooted with her in the very beginning of time are held sacred and silent, protected as myth until she shifts her sleeve in perfect time and perfect reason to impart what may be in danger of being lost forever. Until then, it slumbers in silence with the sun.

    Under that ancient silence, the dunes begin to speak. The sand and wind begin to whisper, manifesting from their restless horizon a single pale falcon passing through a silver-blue sky. They watch proudly under the spell of her freedom as she rises higher. Higher. She sublimates slowly, as if into the legend of imagination, to tell their story once again.

    Through a modern roar, a polished Bedouin man worn well into his eighties seemed out of place and confused as he fought his way against a loud, bustling surge of careless passengers pushing their way with empty faces through

2

Heathrow. He escaped the crowd and sank wearily in the last empty chair, politely acknowledging an eternally inconvenienced, glaring girl plugged into earbuds, iPad, and a measured social-media existence next to him. His heavily lined, travel-weary features softened as he caught a glimpse of a man and his teenage son walking past him, carrying fly rods and Orvis bags. Excited about their journey together, the father smiled proudly and clapped his son's shoulder. The son responded with the sheepish smile of a boy prided as they were swallowed by the crowd. The gate attendant jarred the elderly man back into the misfit of his surroundings with careless volume, announcing the initial boarding. As he moved slowly toward the gate, he marveled at the immensity of the machine that would carry him home.

    As the man watched the skies change from the opulence of his window, a sweet-faced and distantly familiar airline attendant asked if she could get anything to make him more comfortable. She smiled as he asked for a blanket and presented him with two, one black and one red. With a wink, she offered both. He stared hard at the dark-red blanket; studied her for a moment; and slowly, deliberately accepted it. With the troubled dexterity of storied hands, he removed the plastic and thumbed the red fleece, then smoothed it over his forearm, lost in thought. As he watched through his airplane window, the setting sun warmed rolls of clouds, shading them the color of sand dunes. Comforted, the man wrapped himself in red, smiling as he closed his eyes.

2.

A rifle shot echoed beneath the sunset. Through the reverberations, an oryx exploded over the clean edge of a sand dune, bounding with the full strength of his life toward the rise of another dune. The long spikes of his vertical black horns disappeared easily behind it just as Rashid appeared, chasing him. Seeing the tallow beast crest lightly over another dune silenced by desert and distance, his shoulders dropped in defeat. With the force of anger belonging only to a teenager, he yelled, kicked the sand in disgust, and turned around.

Scanning the still sculptures of grand dunes casting vermillion into the last lavender of sunset, his breath flashed, caught in alarm. He was alone. He whirled to scan behind him, but the slow rises of sand, identical in his panic, told him nothing. He closed his eyes to focus himself, and with his second calming breath, a tendril of breeze still warm from the day curled softly around him. As it grew, it carried whispers growing into melodic hints of prayer. His father's prayer. He followed it to the crest of his oryx's grand dune, and he spotted a single tree with a small glint of flame next to it. His sigh began with relief and slowly ended laced with humiliation. Shuffling with shame, he made his way toward the small light holding against the grand advance of night.

A brass coffeepot settled into the coals of a fire beside a small black tent as Rashid walked to it. A jasmine-colored camel swung her elegant head to him and studied him like a big sister with grand black eyes fringed heavily with lashes. Al Rabea. He put his hand on her shoulder, stalling perhaps, gathering himself before stepping to the fire. She knew more of his history than he did, having been a constant presence in it. He had no memory of life without her and her habit of refusing to settle until camp was made. Al Rabea resting was a sign of safety and high comfort. She was home. As she swung her head back to look toward the light, Rashid's shoulders dropped, and he stepped slowly to the fire and the figure seated beside it.

    His father didn't look up. Wordlessly he reached into a small pouch, pulled out a date, and handed it to his son. He pulled the brass pot from the embers; poured an elegantly slight stream of black liquid into a fine, tiny porcelain cup that was unusually delicate in its surroundings; passed it to the lad with a poetry of statement; and turned to the fire in thought.

    "The right thing will come easily to you, Rashid," he said, "but these things that do not are still necessary." He looked at his son with patience and offered his understanding with a gentle gesture to the place next to him by the fire, then handed him another date. They sat for a moment, cross-legged on mats in the sand, as the stars began their emergence. Rashid's father lifted a small dish of melted butter, softly spoke a prayer of gratitude, and they ate together in silence.

    As a great night sky wrapped around the fire, warming their place together in the world, they poured coffee from the brass pot, set out a leather board game, and settled in as they had nearly every evening in Rashid's memory.

    "Perhaps it's not your eyesight failing your aim, but wisdom. That you must grow to know through discipline and the building of skill," his father said through the friendly silence. "Your rifle, Rashid, like any instrument, is an extension of your own respect. Once you feel your own balance and justice with the truth of nature, your shot will be fearless and true. Until then," he admonished with marked, heavy distance and sadness, "a trigger can never be unpulled." Rashid looked at him wide-eyed, wondering at this furrowed expression he had seen before, stamped with a history, a story never told, and wondered if he would ever be such a man. "So you see, you're wise to know it's a grave responsibility." Rashid's father sipped his coffee and looked into the fire. "Once you learn it, and learn it you must, perhaps I will show you another way." His eyes went distant, disappearing into memory. Catching himself, he straightened, shifted diligently to the present, and looked at Rashid with a stretch and a playful glint.

"Trouble is that such a thing is required to earn a wife worth having, and it had better improve because the requirement for finding a wife who can shoot for you or becoming the family of a sheikh so you don't have to shoot unless you want to is far out of your reach, my son." His handsome face betrayed him, cracking into the glint of an escaped smirk and lighting into a shining glimmer of Rashid's beloved father. They laughed into the evening as they bested each other with the board game. Truly they were home there beside the tree, growing smaller in the embrace of an ocean of sand.

6

3.

In the fuchsia and gold of dawn, father and son worked in perfect rhythm, rolling up their black goat-hair tent and tucking it among their belongings, packed carefully with balance on their beloved Al Rabea. She had walked patiently alongside his father all of Rashid's life. Today she was restless. Unusual for her. To her mild protest, they carefully laid a few ornate woven trappings over her saddle, a finishing gesture that was a sign of their regard for her. Rashid's father touched the trappings with familiar distance and affection.

"Blessed family." He patted the camel warmly. "God's gift, Rashid. There is an old lesson in her loyalty."

With effort, they coaxed her to walk a few strides from the tree, and a movement in the desert caught Rashid's attention. He stopped, and his father joined him in scanning the distance. Al Rabea's agitation grew to a pitch, and Rashid's father followed her attention to the west. He squinted and grew grave. Rashid looked hard to the east, and from the sunrise and mirrored mercury manifested blackening spikes and the shape of a grand oryx. Rashid grabbed his father's arm, directing his gaze. As they looked, the animal separated from the sunrise, creating his own light as his color shifted, transmuting to that of a new pearl.

They looked for a moment, caught in awe. In a smooth instant, Rashid's father drew the rifle from Al Rabea's saddle, glancing west.

"That is a voice from the desert, Rashid. A sign of its protection and nobility."

Rashid took the rifle from his father and smiled at him.

"Balance. Justice and respect." His voice seemed lyrical and ageless, somehow sounding like the breeze and sand. "Go. Quickly." He clapped Rashid's shoulder. "Never leave God waiting when he gives you a gift."

Rashid moved swiftly, predator-like, toward the oryx. He was nearly fluid as he moved below the crests of the dunes, stalking his prey. It seemed, for once, that he was getting it right. Thinking of his father's pride, he tilted his rifle over the apex of a dune, using it as a rest as he breathed and sighted. The rifle shook, and he whispered, "I'm balanced. I'm just. I'm balanced…" The magnificent white oryx raised his head slowly and stared unblinkingly at Rashid, holding him there, cast solidly in time. They both breathed. Their eyes were the same. Rashid saw kings and his ancestors there. He saw his childhood in the desert. He saw his mother. In slow motion, the liquid disappeared behind black lashes. The oryx blinked.

A shot echoed from the distance. The oryx blinked again and pounded away with the crashing, hard, halting tempo of Rashid's heartbeat. Rashid turned in the direction of the shot to see his father slowly fall to his knees. He slumped into a figure wearing a long deep-red *ghutrah* over his head and dropped to the ground. The figure turned from him as Rashid scrambled in a breathless, voiceless panic toward his father while the desert held him fast. He couldn't scream, and the sand seemed to hold his legs as if in a nightmare.

As he reached the tree, Rashid watched two camels trotting away to the horizon. The aching groans and bleats of Al Rabea's protest disappeared with them as the man in red rode the other without looking back.

"Stay with me. Do not chase them." Through Rashid's breathless fury scrambling to chase them, the clear, solid voice of his father cut into his awareness. He spoke with the last of his strength. Rashid looked down at his father and dropped to him in confusion. His father mustered the strength to touch his son's handsome, anguished face, then touched his wound with the gravity of realization.

"Listen to me, my son…" he whispered. "As you love me, I forbid you to avenge this. Swear it to me."

"How can I not?" Rashid protested.

His father, nearly gone, stopped him.

"Rashid, a life spent in revenge, my dear son, is a life wasted. I should have taught you. I didn't have time. The desert, she protects you. You must hear it." As his eyes began their departure, the silhouette of a falcon passed through the morning sky behind his son's stricken face. His eyes widened in realization, and he forced himself back to his son with a new firmness as he gathered wisdom from death.

"Fahad. My brother is Fahad. He doesn't know. But he knows your story. Balance. Just…remember."

His hand on Rashid's cheek went slack, and Rashid felt his father's life leave him. Rashid shook his head in disbelief and shock. He raised his face to the sky, confused, denying, weeping and praying in savage, inconsolable anguish, utterly alone and growing smaller in face of the vast giants around him. Had his eyes been open, he might have seen the falcon passing high overhead.

4.

The small, scruffy tree appeared to cling to life without reason in that desperate place. It lived at the mercy and whim of the wind and slowly lumbering giants surrounding it. Against them it was insignificant, unlikely. With its scarcity of hard leaves, it appeared on the slide into death, as it should be for its presumption to exist in such a place. Yet there it was. With no choice but to live or die with its circumstance, it dutifully pulled scant molecules of water from the desert night for what leaves it could afford to serve its purpose. Cleverly, by that high price, it offered shade to nesting houbara and a marking place for oryx and small antelope to gather. Perhaps out of respect for its toughness and commerce, perhaps to keep itself company, the desert had given it a wind shadow to make its honorable and ageless living.

12

5.

Rashid woke draped over a graceful mound of stones next to the tree, and in that moment, the oblivion of sleep faded with agony into reality, new tears darkening lines of salt and the stain of blood drying on his face. He placed a few more stones on the pile to excuse his loss and his lingering and stepped back.

He looked hard at his father's grave as the morning wore toward day around him. The desert around him grew empty and incalculable without his father. He sank to the pile of rocks, willing himself to become one of them and stay there with his father. The shadow of a flying bird flicked through the sun, and he opened his eyes to the trail left by Al Rabea. The anguish in his face shifted to stone and determination. He tightened his cartridge belt and water skin, slung his rifle over his shoulder, and following the two camel tracks, he walked into the heart of the desert without looking back. As he grew small in the distance, a tiny fox feathered to the mound. After some investigation, she curled up on top of it and watched him go.

For days, Rashid moved alone through the desert, following the trail left by the two camels. Struggling with desert skills that should have been with him at birth and were learned from his patient father, he went through the movements his father had always made and felt incapable. A fraud. The movements themselves were sharp reminders of his father and of his reality. Through his slow pursuit, the trail softened and eventually dissolved into the desert. He walked anyway, suffering through bitterly cold desert nights wrapped only in his ghutrah. He tried to shoot small game but couldn't bring himself to pull the trigger. He managed to catch and skin a rabbit but dropped it, fouling most of it with sand. He pulled the last date out of his pouch and looked at it. Another mark of his hunger and loneliness as desert consequence loomed. He swallowed the last of his water as he continued to slog, a single silhouette along one of thousands of dunes and rises in the desert. At dawn, shivering savagely, he rose to pray.

Exhausted beyond reason by hunger and circumstance, Rashid aimed at a small antelope. He watched it down the long barrel as it softly pawed the sand, nosing for something once green and flicking its tail as it moved from possibility to possibility. Through his delirium, he found he was jealous of the creature. It didn't suffer. It wasn't alone. It browsed through its morning, sustained as comfortably as it ever had been, knowing and living by merit of its own existence. It merely was. He shook and breathed but couldn't shoot. A circle of breeze cast sand into Rashid's face. As he blinked, the animal looked up with a start and leaped lightly away. In fury, Rashid shot the rifle in the air, then hurled it. He turned around and froze, then dropped flat to the sand, still but for the hard thumping of his heart. A camel train silhouetted across the horizon stopped at the sound of his rifle. The camels lurched their high loads slowly to a halt, unsettling to their long daily habit. By their purpose, it was much akin to halting commerce and received similar complaint.

Thinking he was unseen, Rashid scanned the line for a red ghutrah. He watched and flattened himself as three men gathered at the front of the train, pointed in his direction, and began to walk toward him. Rashid backed down the rise and retreated quickly, low, nearly stalking. He rounded a small dune, inched his way to the top where he could watch them, and realized with a start that they were walking cautiously toward his rifle, stuck standing barrel-first in the sand. They were dressed like his father, their chests crossed with water skins and pouches, one of them with a line of bullets along his sash, all with curved knives in their belts.

    As two of the men scanned around them, one of them pulled the rifle from the sand, inspected it, and looked straight toward Rashid. The man's leathered face was thoughtful, old for its years, and in contrast to his companions' grave expressions, watchful, certain of their danger, his seemed to carry a smart, knowing smile, though the muscles showed nothing. Strangely, he reached into his pouch, pulled out a few dates, handed one to each of his companions, took a bite, and turned to walk back toward the camel train carrying the rifle. Rashid watched his rifle, and all eyes focused on the break in their rhythm. The smiling man slid the rifle into his saddle and, with diligent purpose and attention only on the road ahead, resumed the long walk once again, while the others quietly searched where Rashid hid.

    Aching with hunger, Rashid followed, stalking at first, then shuffling as the distance between them grew. Finally, watching them go with his ability to survive, he stopped, shoulders drooping. The leader, aware of him already, glanced back in thought and studied the white figure for a moment, tiny in that place. He reached down, gathered a handful of sand, lifted it above his head, and released it slowly into a veil caught by a light desert breeze, declaring their peaceful intentions.

    All eyes were on him as he approached apprehensively, remaining quiet as the leader greeted him, introducing himself as Faisal. His father had always done the talking, with an artful balance of disarming warmth and distinct reservation that invited respect but no query. Rashid was tongue-tied. They noted the blood on his clothes and his general state and politely held their questions. A few of them scanned the desert where his tracks originated. Faisal considered him for a long moment. Years of slow study had convinced him of his own instincts. He reached into a pouch and offered him a handful of dates and his water.

"Walk with us today. We'll have coffee when we stop tonight."

Rashid paused, wary. Then he slowly, gratefully accepted them and the protection they represented. For the moment, it seemed, he was safe.

6.

"Is there a camel market where you are going?" Rashid asked.

Faisal stopped in mid pour for a moment, and the others turned their gazes from the fire holding their coffee, for the first time taking measure of his voice. He and his silence had been a point of curiosity for them. A silent lad with a hollowed face and bloodstains, alone out here in this emptiness carrying an empty water skin, a rifle, and a cartridge belt, had left them uneasy. A note in his voice woke brotherly instincts in most of them but didn't soften their distrust at the danger of his circumstance.

"In the market, are you?" replied Faisal, finishing his politely slight pour. "I might consider selling one of mine if you'd rather not go all the way to Muwaiqih."

"Mine was stolen from me. I need to find her."

Faisal studied him, then looked at the other travelers. He had requested their help without asking.

"How do you intend to pay for your passage?" His question fished for more than the boy's financial liquidity.

Rashid deflated. Thinking, he looked at the game two of the men were playing and missed his father.

"Perhaps he could win it." One of the happier-faced travelers saw the familiarity in Rashid's face and spoke up. He had been moved by Rashid's circumstance from the beginning. "If he has talent enough to beat Saif, I'll hire him to work for me and pay for part of his passage."

"Okay, young friend," said Faisal. "Do you agree to this trial?"

Rashid nodded, filled with quiet hope.

"Fair enough. What do you have of value to contribute for the other part?"

Rashid shoved his sand-infused rifle forward. The men laughed. It was a better thing for everyone to contribute to the remainder of his tariff so a camel would be saved the dead weight of the useless and ugly ornament of his rifle.

They called forward their champion. As Saif entered the firelight, annoyed, anemic, and confident, he puffed and sized up Rashid, who was markedly bigger and infinitely more surprised than he, as they were roughly the same age. He stretched his hands with drama to drum up more reaction from the travelers, cracked his neck, and sat in front of the board. The display and response inspired Saif to place in two cigars intended as gifts for the sheikh and three days' ride on his camel. As he moved to the board, Rashid was caught by one dark face in the firelight, detached, brooding, studying him with more intensity than the others. Rashid shivered. He situated himself in front of the board and looked back for the face, but it had disappeared from the firelight.

The next morning, Rashid rode comfortably in a soft saddle on a particularly large camel with a pocketful of dates and his rifle packed neatly beside him. Saif walked beside the camel, dampened and glowering, floundering a little as he waded through the sand.

"Let's see you win at storytelling," he grumbled.

"I'm grateful for your hospitality, but my legs will get sore if I ride for three days," said Rashid. "Would you mind if we took turns walking?"

Saif looked up at him with some slow measure and smirked despite himself. "Grateful for your hospitality…" He chuckled. "You wouldn't be sore if you were riding Masroor. She floats as though on wings..." Seeing Rashid's curiosity, he puffed a little with importance and paused for theatrical effect. "Masroor is my horse."

Rashid's curiosity warmed to wonder. He had seen horses on the very rare occasion that they went to town. His father had always unpacked Al Rabea near the horses with instructions that Rashid not leave her side. He was fascinated with them. He had watched their bright ears; long, carefully carried tails; and tiny feet move from the basins to the fence where their owners had disappeared into the scattered date palms of town. When they returned, he noted every detail of grooming and saddling and bridling them, watching the horses grow more restless with the progress, keen to rejoin the desert.

"Have you ever ridden?" asked Saif, seeing the thoughts roll across Rashid's face.

Rashid had a vague picture of a smiling horseman lifting him as a young child onto the saddle of a bay mare, and holding the long black mane as the animal stepped gingerly after the kind man, carefully carrying her precious cargo as his father beamed. "Not really," he said softly, lingering on the thought of his father's rare smile.

"Well, you'll have to ride Masroor. She's the fastest in all of the desert...except for my cousin's horse, Malaak." He shook his head. "He's *huge*! And all white. White, white, white. He's mean too. He was supposed to be my father's horse, but he bucked him off and bit him on the backside once. Everybody thought he'd kill that horse in a second, but when he trotted straight to my cousin, my father laughed so hard and said the horse knew his rider, and it wasn't him!

Everybody knows my cousin's the only one he'll let ride him now. And in a race, nobody can beat them...although my father won't let them go in a *real* race, of course. They'd still win, though. I know they would."

Rashid jumped down from the walking camel, stepped into stride with his new friend, and listened contentedly to him rattle on, seemingly without breathing, as he explained everything from the parts of the saddle to the minds of horses as they marched through the great and endless waves of the desert, forgetting, for then, that he felt alone.

7.

The travelers, bonded as tribesmen by the seriousness of their journey, ranged from witty and quirky to elegant and brooding. The dark character from the fire, impeccable, beautiful, and menacing, never uttered a word but studied Rashid even when his eyes weren't on him. He seemed adept and contained, as if his walk with the caravan was only a coincidence of timing rather than his real life.

"Who is that?" Rashid asked Saif as they trudged down the crest of a dune.

"I don't know his name," said Saif, bored. "I don't think anyone has ever heard him say anything. He's just part of the caravan. Has been for years. Kind of comes and goes. They say he can track anything," he half whispered. "Even birds... I just call him the Silent Tribesman. So why were you traveling by yourself?" he asked.

Rashid looked at him, sizing him up to take his measure. "Why are you?" he jousted.

Saif raised a shoulder, ready to spin a yarn.

"His father wanted him to learn about the desert," Faisal interrupted from behind him.

Saif deflated a little, his mystery blown.

"Of course, you know about the desert, don't you?" Faisal asked.

Rashid shrugged.

"If you're going to ride with the caravan, you'll need some skills."

Saif rolled his eyes and looked at Rashid as if he had just been roped into dull reading classes.

The tribesmen took on a reluctant Rashid as a project, alongside Saif, teaching them their secrets of the desert, finding both their young skills the perfect answer to the monotony of their progress across the sand. They read direction, found water through ancient knowledge, and built fires. The Silent Tribesman watched with darkened interest as Rashid shook uncontrollably when he shouldered his rifle. Pretending they hadn't noticed, they graciously moved on to another skill. In the end, to their endless amusement, he surprised them with his one point of mastery: the ability to disappear utterly into a dune. A few of them laughed, figuring that had to be worth something, and nicknamed him Xunfusaa, or Little Beetle. As the journey wore on, under the watch of the travelers, skills Rashid had learned from his father emerged slowly, revealing themselves to his comfort and his sadness.

As evening faded to night, discussions of their progress shifted by habit to story. As they sipped coffee, one by one, each spun a tale. Some spoke of history, some of mythical ocean creatures, and some expounded on the grace and loveliness of the sheikh's family, respectfully, artfully, never mentioning sheikhas they had never seen. Rashid listened with distance, carried with them as each story expanded his world further from the narrow circle of his father and Al Rabea, which had been the sum of his existence. Closing his eyes to imagine his father sitting with him, wondering what his story would have been. He missed him.

"They're finally getting good." Saif plopped down beside him, munching on dates as he listened to a scruffy-faced traveler Rashid hadn't studied, and handed him a date. "We're getting close."

Rashid looked at him curiously. He always seemed to appear the moment Rashid fell into loneliness.

"When we get to town, Faisal will go to meet the sheikh. Traditionally, anyone can go speak with the sheikh, but because of protocol, they have to state their case then wait to be invited. The caravan is only moving through, as always, so by tradition, only one may go with Faisal. They decided the one with the best story will be chosen. It's been going on for weeks!"

One by one, the tribesmen stood among the circle of men sitting in the firelight under the council of stars and there beneath heaven, testing their fates by spinning and weaving each of their tales. The tapestry of them together now took shape with the color of each thread. As each man finished, the others responded with measured regard, good humor, then waited uncomfortably for the next volunteer. Invariably, between each tale, a blanket of expectation fell on Rashid and the vault inside him where his story was kept.

As the caravan drew nearer to the safety of town, the stories turned to darker legends. A quiet, wiry traveler who preferred to walk beside his camel stood with his spectacles in his hand, took a focusing breath, and studied the group. None of them shifted as he looked deep into the fire, assuming that was where his story would be. In a deep and quiet voice, he began his tale with measure and bravery.

"There are places in the desert so empty, their record on maps and memory remain only suggestion, as they have never been crossed nor visited by any human in a thousand years…save for one, whom it houses. A murderer. A godless, blackhearted pariah, a giant riddled with bloodlust." He looked around and gathered seriousness from the grave faces in the firelight. "Makar Samūm."

8.

The expressions of those listening changed and looked to Faisal, the way sailors would look to their captain to stop a story about pirates told while on high seas. Violent poison winds and sea dragons floated among their whispers. Faisal, amused, gestured for the story to go on.

As the storyteller continued, Rashid's gaze was pulled to the Silent Tribesman as a flash of emotion crossed his face. He saw Rashid had caught him, and his eyes again turned to stone.

The broached subject triggered a deluge of stories, nervously told, in the tradition of pirate tales, with each legend of the rise and reason for Makar Samūm's evil more colorful than the last. Most believed him to be a ghost tale to frighten children back to camps and homes before sunset; others took him more gravely. Each story began with a description of a scar-faced giant of a man; a small, one-eyed man; or a horrible, scarred ogre with eyes devoid of a soul, and continued to weave a horror story of his pursuit of a distant member of their families. Some lightened the tenor by telling a spoofed version that drew roars of laughter, mostly celebrating the breaking of tension. Each ended with the same statement: "No man still living has ever seen him, for those who have, he has killed."

"If no one has ever seen him, how do they know what he looks like?" Rashid whispered his skepticism, mostly to himself.

"And over his head, a ghutrah!" chanted Saif as several men dramatically chimed in to the common poem known by all children but Rashid. "Red by the blood of his hundred men slain…!"

Rashid felt the slow drain of blood from his face and his hands. Slow crescendos of his breath and heartbeat roared deliberately through the laughter and men chanting the black nursery rhyme as the image of his father slumping against a man in red paralyzed him as it had before and forced him to see again the red disappearing over the dune behind his dying father, dragging a bleating Al Rabea with him. He stood up, blanched.

The jocose chanting stopped, and the tribesmen turned toward him. Most of them had never heard his voice, and they craned to hear.

"Lay down your story, then, young wanderer!"

Rashid wasn't sure who had said it. Knowing he was his only protector, he wasn't sure what to reveal, so he stood there under their gazes, trying to gather his strategy. They waited. His heart thumped, the only partner who knew his truth with him. There was no escape from it.

Faisal saw his struggle. "How does it begin?"

Rashid looked hard at him, but no words would come. But for the hard drum of Rashid's heart, silence.

"Well, then, how does it end?"

Rashid looked into the fire, steadying himself. "It ends with my killing a man." As it fell from his mouth seemingly of its own accord, he felt a stab as his betrayal of his father took root. The men, some still amused, some grave, watched him as the fire swayed with the desert's evening breath, changing shapes as it changed light.

Faisal gave him more ground. "Does this dead man have a name?" He hesitated, then deliberately handed Rashid a date, along with the protection it represented.

"I don't know his name, but I will before he dies." Rashid suddenly seemed old beyond his years.

"How will you know him?" asked a voice from beyond the fire. "Have you seen his face?"

"He will be wearing a ghutrah, red with the blood of a hundred men and my father, and he will have a camel named Al Rabea, who won't eat or drink until her camp is set and the fire made."

The men went silent. Stupefied. Each of them silently questioned this fairy tale and this quiet lad with eyes that had seen too much. Being men of the desert, they knew the character of truth. Some studied him in awe; some moved away, instinctively distancing themselves from the possibility of attachment. The Silent Tribesman stood, looked with hard tragedy at Rashid, and walked wordlessly away from the fire.

The others stood with the hush of a significant moment while Faisal gripped his shoulder.

"Your purpose is much greater even than the path you see before you."

The tribesmen knew they weren't going to meet the sheikh.

9.

The colors announcing the advance of dawn in the desert write their own music. The ballad of each day is different, brushing with a breeze that promises the sand somewhere is already being warmed and the inevitability of day is as it has always been. There, in the moments before the camels began to stir, Rashid watched it arrive. The breeze folded, and the faint whisper of singing curled around him, much as it did when he was lost in the desert. He studied it and fell into it as it carried the very notes sung by his father. Beyond the rise where they rested was Muwaiqih and the morning prayer that called it to day.

    The camels had brightened days before, but as the tips of date palms grew on the horizon, their rhythm changed with palpable excitement. Rashid ached to turn back to the safety of the desert and to his history. He had been in a city only a few times since he was a very small child, and always with the safety of his gentle father. When he and his father did go, he was generally told to stay in the outskirts with Al Rabea, where somehow it was still safe and known. Now he looked to Saif for advice and distraction, but his friend was nowhere to be found.

    The camels luxuriated in stone troughs of water as their riders unloaded and unsaddled them in the decadent shade of date palms. The men worked quickly, then splashed their faces with water, bright and anxious to go into town themselves. Rashid scanned the other camels stabled there, hoping through pure force of will that Al Rabea would appear among them. He busied himself helping the men, avoiding the inevitable. He stopped to marvel at a few horses softly milling around and lost himself as he watched them delicately nosing for a few stray dates. He wondered where Saif was. He turned to look for him and jumped. The Silent Tribesman was standing beside him, impeccable as always and menacing. He walked away, then gestured Rashid to come with him. It wasn't a suggestion. He looked again for Saif and Faisal to no avail. The kindly traveler who first had challenged Rashid to a board game smiled sadly, patted his shoulder, and nodded to him to go with the Silent Tribesman. Rashid picked up his rifle and water skin and reluctantly followed him into the city. A look back to see his fellow travelers watching him go was his only goodbye.

10.

Rashid had to trot to keep up with the tall tribesman as he turned down palm-lined alleyways, past shop fronts and irrigation troughs with water moving lazily along them without concern that it was in the desert. Masked emerald birds lit and watched their progress. Rashid wondered at them and felt a thump of nervousness, realizing they had surely seen the sheikh too.

They walked through fragrances he couldn't identify. Sweet, comfortable smoke from a *shisha*. Cardamom and coffee, and the moist smell of ripe dates on palms lingering with flowers and various kinds of oud wafting from stores and small buildings, inspiring varying degrees of joy and protection for the occupants and telling stories of their nature on their behalf. Curious faces emerged and whispered together as the handsome young Bedouin and his mordant protector walked past, then studied them with curious measure as they stopped for the Silent Tribesman to point and hand over a coin for food.

Rashid stopped as they walked toward a bright opening between the dense lines of palms. The entire opening was filled with a grand, dark door that took its shape from the grace of elegant Islamic arches, meeting in a perfect center so they could point to heaven. They walked forward through the palms and into the evening sun. From velvety green grass, great vermillion walls rose before them. Perfectly clean, the color of the wild dunes beyond, they stretched from side to side of the great door. Great wooden beams stood through, hinting at a grand structure beyond them, and above the beams, the walls were celebrated with rounded merlon teeth atop long, solid parapets. Rashid watched an emerald bird fly over the wall and ached and dreaded, wondering what the bird saw there. He was at once overwhelmed with apprehension.

"No." Something outside Rashid pulled him back to the desert, away from what existed beyond the door. The Silent Tribesman stopped. "I can do what I need to do without the help of a sheikh or a town or you or anyone." He started to back away as adrenaline mounted. "You cannot force me. I'll...I'll ride with the caravan like you. Eventually, I'll find him...The desert will show me; I just have to be patient." He turned and set off on his retreat into the alley between the palms.

"You must learn not to fear but respect the thing that cannot be undone." The Silent Tribesman's voice was deep, resonating with story and worldliness and education. It followed and captured Rashid. "You are a son of the desert, Rashid. This is the way of your desert...Bringing your story to be heard by our sheikh honors your father and sets you on your path with the grace of being right to follow and find what you must do. Balance with justice first, and what is right that gives you life will always follow."

Rashid stared, stupefied.

"Hide from it as I did, and you will become an empty man, angrily waiting for death." He breathed. "You must live in the time brought to you."

Rashid stared at him, dumbfounded. Was he real? Could others in the oasis see him, or was he a ghost of the ancestors? Where he saw only menace before, he now also glimpsed wisdom, disappointment, and solitary torment. He understood and recognized it because it was a thing of the desert. Without another word, he followed the tribesman to the gate and listened as he rumbled Faisal's name.

The great studded doors thumped and cracked in the center and allowed them in to see the first sliver of what the bird had seen. As they thundered slowly together, closing the bustle of the oasis behind them, the two travelers were met with a new world, previously unimaginable yet still infused with the familiar peace of the desert, receiving them with safety and an unexpected feeling of belonging and welcome speaking of home.

The delicacy of the garden defied anything Rashid had conjured to dream. He was helpless in his wonder. His world had previously been colored in sepia, blue, and sunset, marked by the red of Al Rabea's saddle blanket and, occasionally, the dusty verdant watercolor of date palms. Here the great walls felt like his dunes, but these, dressed in climbing green and marked with clean tiny white trumpets celebrating dusk with velvety fragrance, guarded different secrets. He could feel it. Lines of fuchsia and violet and periwinkle blossoms atop slender green towers accompanied the walkway, and the emerald bird alit in a tall shrub beside them, a happy and proud host, escorting them through his garden as lamps and lanterns were being lit to warmly greet the advancing evening.

The Silent Tribesman stopped, motioned for Rashid to wait, and continued toward the structures alone. Rashid was glad for the moment alone to take in this world. The emerald bird flitted in front of him and rose to a palm, where he settled near a second bird, strategically placing himself so she could admire his grand spiked tail feather. A soft motion continued below him as a nearly apparitional figure moved like liquid through silks and fabrics the same verdigris tinged green as the bird, materializing from the magic of her surroundings and caught softly for a moment in the shadow of the lanterns. Rashid was lost in the movement as she held him helpless in a clear and innocent gaze, and an eternity fled past. He tore his eyes from her to the bird, mostly to prove to himself that they were separate beings. She looked up at the bird. "He's my lookout." She said with a smirk. The pain of it washed across his face as she melted again into the garden, with the soft bells of giggles from her friends in the shadows mingling with the sound of water trickling into a stone basin somewhere beyond. Rashid stood as though he had felt the sun for the first time and then watched it fade away into night. After the sound and fragrance faded through the garden and into the gold light of the white structure beyond it, Rashid became aware that the Silent Tribesman was watching him knowingly, patiently waiting for his faculties to return before walking him along an open corridor to the door of the majlis, where the sheikh waited.

11.

Warmly lit, the majlis welcomed with its own austere temperament. Its temperature alone spoke of its place there, with a clear understanding that it remained constant against the rhythms of seasons and days. Even as Rashid stepped into its door, marked with the soft curls of the oud burning beside it to welcome and cast away all but wisdom, the room breathed in the freshness of dusk and promised to remain a place of comfort against the oncoming chill of night and comfortably stage the business at hand. The floors were covered with ornately patterned blue rugs, and dozens of blue-cushioned seats marked three sides of the room. A few men milled around a square stove with elegant arched, brass coffeepots resting in mounds of coals.

Rashid, looking around a little nervously, spotted Faisal, who acknowledged him with a nod. The Silent Tribesman locked gazes with a taller, elegant man among them and gestured quietly toward Rashid. The man swept forward to greet Rashid with the warmth of a relative. The Silent Tribesman then turned from a brooding study of Rashid to walk wordlessly into the night.

The sheikh's face was kind, angular, and handsome. His eyes looked like Arabic writing, the edges scrolled downward into the soft lines of a lifetime of smiling, framing the clarity of eyes that revealed greater depths of secrets and knowing than his greeting, which was measured perfectly to ease the bewildered desert lad before him. In a moment, the sheikh took in the state of Rashid, and his protective fatherly instincts washed over him. He patted the boy warmly on his shoulder and invited him to sit beside him, offered him fruit, and poured a tiny coffee for him from the long, graceful spout of the brass pot as the others settled around them. Rashid stopped as he spotted Saif, crisp in elegant, fresh robes, settling in a few seats away from the sheikh. He smirked knowingly at Rashid and shrugged, rolling his eyes.

"You have had quite a journey, young man." Unable to find a reply, Rashid nodded. The sheikh studied him for a moment, considering the value of small talk. "Most would argue that Makar Samūm is nothing but a legend. That a story like yours is about gaining attention from me."

The air of attention dropped to wide-eyed focus as Rashid looked at the great sheikh's face directly in surprise. The image of his father sinking to the sand flashed through him as he stood, failing the young man's effort to conceal his response. The other men in the room hung on every gesture.

"But the truth is, you and I share a common claim on him."

Rashid looked at him, straight and hard, and the sheikh saw a depth of strength and mutual understanding belying his age. He allowed silence to fill the space between them as he sipped his coffee.

"He murdered my brother, you see."

The energy in the room stirred, though no one moved through the silence held by the pure strength of thought of their leader.

"What do you want?" the sheikh asked bluntly.

Rashid's voice was clear. "I want my camel, Al Rabea. I want my belongings."

The sheikh nodded, a little bored, holding the silence for Rashid and the truth he was clearly holding.

"And I want to kill Makar Samūm and avenge my father."

The sheikh seemed satisfied. Carefully hidden within his nod was a quiet, knowing exchange with Faisal. "Makar Samūm is a criminal of the highest order, Rashid. Some of the greatest of my men have gone against him and lost. Not one man who has seen his face has lived. Not one. That truth has magnified him, I'm afraid."

Rashid remained steady. Unfazed under his eyes. The sheikh breathed deeply, then deliberately poured Rashid another elegant slip of coffee and personally handed him a date.

"Leave me alone with my children."

Most of the room gathered themselves and rose to leave. Saif, a smaller boy, and the girls remained. Rashid, still with a date in his cheek, rose to leave.

"Rashid, that means you, my boy." The sheikh gestured to the seat beside him, and they waited as the room cleared. "I'm very sorry you have lost your father. Tell me, what was his name?"

"Majid..." Rashid hung his head, embarrassed.

The sheikh studied him slowly, working carefully through this mystery that sat beside him, considering the protection of a father who would withhold his family and name from his son, even in death. "Did he say anything to you before he died?"

"He forbade me to avenge his death. He asked me to swear to it."

The sheikh gave him time as Rashid fought back the image of his father.

"He told me that a life spent in revenge is a life wasted and that the desert will protect me if I can hear it."

Saif and the other children looked at their feet. The girls' eyes welled for him.

"He also said I have an uncle. Fahad."

Saif and the others brightened and looked up at their father, whose eyes had widened as he looked hard at the lad. "Have you never met this uncle?" the sheikh asked gently.

Rashid looked down and shook his head.

"Well"—the sheikh stirred the coals—"if it is Fahad the falconer, we will know soon enough. I'll send for him with no news of this." He flashed a gentle and admonishing glance to the children. "God may declare so Himself if he is your uncle. Until He does, this is our secret." He smiled. "Until then, you'll stay here with us. Tomorrow, I'll show you something that will brighten your day. Rest and feel safe." He clapped Rashid warmly on the shoulder with telling sorrow and understanding.

"There is a story before us, you and me, young Rashid...and much depends upon it."

12.

The lilting call to prayer echoed through the early morning before dawn, easing Rashid gently into this foreign world. He remembered the pieces of it rolling through the desert to fold softly around camels and travelers, nudging them through the last of their rest. He wondered whether they were there now and could hear it. It sounded different than it had the day before. Perhaps because it found its way to him by echoes of town and date trees and palace walls and the Little Green Bee-Eaters that joined in the end, as it ushered them into day as well. He thought of his uncle, whoever he was, and studied for a moment the question of why he never had known about him. It was simply his life that his world consisted of his father, al Rabea, and the desert, and he had never questioned it. He listened to the movements of the palace grounds and wondered whether she was out there somewhere.

A light tapping at his door startled him. He breathed for a moment before quietly opening the door. A sleepy Saif stood there. "Come on. My father wants to see you."

They walked across the family courtyard as Rashid's emerald bird flitted by them, landing with them to preen and watch their progress. Rashid looked up to see the sheikh studying them with a smile.

"Not even a month in the desert could force mornings into your nature, Saif?"

Saif yawned. "No, Baba."

"Rashid, when is the last time you have been into a mews?"

"A mews, sir?"

A flash of confusion passed the sheikh's face, followed by a grin. "If falconry is in your bones, we can suspect Fahad is your uncle and you will feel much at home." He led Rashid through an ornate, airy door.

"These are like my children," he said as they stepped into a room.

Rashid's jaw dropped, and his breath caught as he realized what he was seeing. Lines of falcons of various shapes rested easily with hoods and jesses tethered to elegant green block perches. The sheikh grinned as he reached down, picked up a small Lanner falcon, and removed her hood for Rashid to see. For the second time in as many days, Rashid felt as though he were seeing the sun for the first time.

The sheikh grinned knowingly. "Let us suspect that our Fahad is yours also."

He handed the cuff with the great falcon to Rashid, who stood in amazement that the movement and weight and otherworldly presence of her felt like home. She turned to study him with black eyes, looking through into another part of him.

"All of these are Fahad's birds. He brought them to me. Let's hope he'll finally bring me a Saker this time."

Rashid tried to be polite through his hypnosis. "Yes, sir..." He stared. "What is a Saker, sir?"

The sheikh looked at him in amazement. "You'll know soon enough, my lad." He laughed. "If you do, we may soon be family..."

As the sheikh carefully closed the door to the mews and rattled it to check it, Saif elbowed Rashid. "C'mon. It smells in there. I want to show you Masroor."

"You go to the gate and meet us, Saif. We'll be there shortly."

Saif shrugged and trotted away. The sheikh walked with Rashid for a moment in silence around a corner, down a passageway spilling with morning sun through star-shaped lattices of long *mashrabiya*, and toward an arched wooden gate where Saif was headed. In a lowered voice he finally spoke. "Rashid, this is very important only for me to know. Once you answer this, you must not answer it again to anyone. Do you understand? Not to Saif, not to anyone but me."

Rashid nodded, wide-eyed.

"It is also very important that you tell me the truth." He paused for it to sink in. "Did you see the face of Makar Samūm, the man who killed your father?"

"No, sir. I didn't."

"Did he see you? Did he hear you?"

Rashid fell into the flash of memory, slamming hard into the image of the desert holding him breathless, unable to scream. "No, sir." He said, swallowing hard. "I was too far away."

"Why?"

"There was a white oryx…I was stalking. I heard the shot and saw him…the red ghutrah…" He squeezed his eyes shut.

The sheikh studied him for a moment, put a fatherly arm over his shoulder, and walked toward Saif, who was waiting impatiently by the gate.

13.

Given the time, Rashid would have studied the gate with fascination, but Saif shoved it, banging it open with announcement. The horses on the other side of it snorted, trotted two steps with their tails in the air, and looked to see what vermin had disturbed them before going back to the high stone basin where they had been. The movement continued behind them as two figures slipped through a door on the other side of the yard beside the arched openings to the stalls. Saif rolled his eyes. "She saw you, you know. Last night. My cousin…"

Rashid snapped to focus on him. "Your cousin?"

"Sure. You know, the one who rides Malaak, that monster over there. I told you about him."

Rashid craned to see an elegant creature the color of a clear moon, much bigger than the rest of the rainbow of dainty horses around him, flatten his ears and flip his head to move them from where he wanted to be at the basin, munching on dates soaked in camel's milk. Saif snorted. "Pfft. Whoever wants to marry her is going to have to pass the test with *that* thing…Here's my horse, Masroor…Rashid!"

Rashid tore his eyes from the elegant creature to Saif, who was scratching the withers of an angled bay with a white line down the center of her face from her ears to her upper lip. As Saif scratched, her grand liquid eyes closed, her lip stretched, and she curled her swan-shaped neck around Saif, who laughed and scratched more. In her glazed luxury, the horse lifted her back leg forward, catching Saif in a horselike hug. When he stopped, Masroor shook like a dog and nosed around Saif's hand. Saif opened it to reveal the date he had brought as a treat. With his arm over Masroor's neck, Saif pointed to all the horses, mentioning their names and some of their finer traits.

"Do you want to ride?" he asked.

"I've never ridden a horse," Rashid said.

"I know. You told me."

"Maybe someday," Rashid dodged.

"You'll never get to talk to my cousin if you don't." Saif smirked. "Her name is Salama, by the way," he said under his breath.

"Where is a saddle?" Rashid asked.

"You learn to ride first. Then you can have a saddle...They just get in the way anyway." Without waiting for Rashid to think, Saif reached down and laced his hands. "Step here and swing your leg over his back...No, your other foot." With no saddle and no bridle on Masroor, Saif helped launch Rashid awkwardly onto her back.

The view from up there was strange to Rashid, who was used to riding a camel. There was nothing substantial in front of him. He pulled up his knees, and Masroor's ear went back to sort out what was going on. "Let your legs down, reach your feet to the ground, and don't wrap your arms around her neck. She'll put her head down, and you'll be stuck in the desert by yourself." Without waiting for him to adjust, Saif pushed Masroor into a walk. "Sit in the middle of her."

Within a few strides, Rashid found a balance and started to understand the rhythm of the walk. Masroor followed Saif dutifully, then eventually became bored and walked with her passenger to the basin to nose around for a wayward date or two. Rashid patted her neck awkwardly, and Saif squinted up at him.

"Well, it's a little better than how well you shoot," Saif said with a grin. "Told you you'd like it."

Behind the mashrabiya, three girls watched and giggled quietly, one of them with a hint of admiration.

45

14.

Rashid sat anxiously. His new clothes made him a little careful and self-conscious, but he was glad to be able to blend in with Saif and his brothers just then. He anchored his gaze away from the beautiful girl, but for him, she filled the majilis even from her discreet place in it with her sisters.

Rashid's heart skipped a beat when the doors opened for a moment before a figure appeared. Was this really his uncle? A perfectly groomed, handsome young man strode into the room dramatically, as if he belonged, with a grand smile on his face. The sheikh greeted him with warmth and familiarity. Rashid studied the side of him from where he sat, and caught Salama's obscured face beyond him turned stony. The sheikh himself poured coffee for his guest and inquired about his journey there. The room was thick with anticipation.

"Fahad, my friend, I didn't know you had a brother..."

Fahad stopped hard, and his face fell, changing it. He thought before speaking. "I had many, Your Highness," he said sadly. "They're all gone. I lost them long ago."

"I'm sad to hear that." The sheikh poured him another touch of coffee to change the subject. "Have you heard the news? Another man has been killed by Makar Samūm."

Fahad's expression darkened. "No, sir. I'm surprised to hear this. Generally when he strikes it's all anyone can talk about. Do you know anything of it or how they're trying to stop him?"

The sheikh stirred the coals for a moment.

"Did anyone see him this time?"

"The murdered man, called Majid, told his son as he died that he had a brother called Fahad. Is it possible...would that be you, my friend?" The sheikh, studying his expression gestured to Rashid, and Fahad, the shock of the news washing across his face, whirled to see his nephew.

Rashid, seeing the man's face, stood up, a little dumbfounded. His father's face was among the younger features. Fahad walked slowly to him, grasped both his shoulders, and looked hard at him. Words wouldn't come. He was Rashid's elder mirror.

"My brother Majid is dead..."

Rashid looked down, then back to Fahad, who was struggling to make sense of the moment.

"Majid had a son. You're his son. Do you not know of me?"

Rashid shook his head, and Fahad, devastated, embraced the boy with the might of loss.

"Yes, you are, aren't you?" He stared. "You'll come live with me."

The sheikh, sad and stoic, cleared emotion from his throat. Rashid, without meaning to, caught his kind, nearly black eyes brimming with tears.

15.

As he rode through the safety of the palace gates with his uncle on Saif's irascible camel, Rashid craned back to wave a small and final farewell to the sheikh and to his one friend. Somewhere in the green behind them was his emerald bird and Salama. The great doors closed between them, and they made their way out to the desert and uncertainty in silence.

Rashid was relieved to be in the open desert again and glanced as often as he dared at the distant, deeply troubled face of his uncle and the hooded falcon he carried on his arm. His fascination was palpable.

"Did your father never teach you falconry?" Rashid looked down. "It's the noblest of fine arts." The subject itself was a warm light for Fahad. "Once we're out of town, she will hunt and catch our supper as though we are kings, and you'll understand."

As they rode, Fahad felt the keel of the falcon as the first study of her readiness and removed her hood. She roused and looked directly at Rashid with ancient black eyes that turned the color of his father's coffee as she swung her gaze to the desert sun. She bobbed her head as she saw something invisible to Rashid, and in a schooled movement originating from them both, Fahad cast her into flight. As she circled upward, carrying them somehow in her freedom, Fahad noted Rashid's fascination. "There are those who would claim to be falconers, but it isn't in their heart. Like love, it's a truth that once you know it, you'll never forget it." He smiled. "Like love, it teaches discipline, character, and respect." He watched as she rocketed downwind and folded her wings to flip herself in the breeze as though stretching. "To me, it's the air."

As if to punctuate Fahad's comment, the falcon circled for a moment, then tilted into a stoop. Her speed was far faster than a fall, and Rashid grimaced as she neared the ground, unwilling to watch her slam into the sand and die. On the ground, a bustard exploded from the brush in a bid to escape. The falcon struck, and the bustard was knocked to the ground for good. She tilted back to it and hit it, binding to it. With a twist of her beak, her prey was killed. She looked up and stood nobly, her talons gripping the bustard as Fahad approached. He picked her up and admired her prey, picking it up with a respect that surprised Rashid. Fahad rewarded her with the tastiest piece of the bustard and placed the rest of it in his quarry bag.

Then he cast her off again, and as she slipped back into the sky, the last of the troubled distance on his face washed into admiration and quiet joy. "She is the best I have had this year."

Rashid listened quietly. His curiosity brimmed.

"I capture wild falcons, train them to hunt with me, then sell the best to the sheikh. I fly some for myself and release the rest."

They walked as he spoke, and the falcon slowed, waiting-on with them.

"This is an important year. I need to pay the dowry for a niece of our sheikh."

The falcon's attitude shifted as she spotted something. "What do you think, Nephew?"

The falcon stooped again and killed another bustard.

"I think I was born to find this," Rashid said breathlessly as they ran toward the falcon and her prey. He stopped. "I may never need to shoot my rifle again."

Fahad looked at him as though guarded for a joke, but seeing Rashid's seriousness, his handsome face broke into an enormous empathetic grin, and he waved Rashid to join him at the quarry. Again Fahad offered reverence to the bustard and rewarded the falcon with the choicest morsel as Rashid watched, unable to see enough of it.

"How much is a dowry?" Rashid asked rather quietly.

It was the last thing Fahad had expected to hear from him, but he held his reaction carefully. "Why? Do you have your eye on someone already? You want to be the son-in-law to a sheikh too, do you?"

Rashid shrugged and smiled for the first time in what seemed like years. His smile was the same as his uncle's. "I don't care who she is. I just want to meet her."

"Perhaps you'll have your chance at my wedding. It may be your only chance, so you'll need to make your mark before then."

Frenzied, witless barking greeted them as their camels strode into the yard of Fahad's home and the decadent shade of a lone date palm. The cause of the racket rounded the corner, revealing itself to be a mongrel half the size of the bark and twice as cowardly, whose charms rested solely in his homeliness. Fahad chased him off, but the dog followed them sheepishly. They rounded the back of Fahad's house to a line of huts. A boy appeared from a shaded doorway with a half-sewn leather falcon hood in his hand. He was the same age as Rashid but, much like the mongrel, had a sense of anemia about him. He looked from Fahad to Rashid with confusion as they were introduced.

"Mohammed, this is Rashid," Fahad said. "He's my nephew. Mohammed here is working to become a falconer so he can train for a sheikh one day, aren't you?"

Mohammed was measured and silent as he greeted Rashid, stepping back as Fahad pushed the door open past him. They walked in to see a line of hooded falcons sitting majestically in a row. Taking in Rashid's awe, Fahad stepped in to bask in it for a moment and expand his hero's role.

"Rashid here will be joining us to trap falcons on the salt pans this year. I'll show you everything a young falconer needs to know." He clapped his hand on Rashid's shoulder a little awkwardly as blackness welled uncontrollably onto Mohammed's already jealous face.

16.

The morning prayer echoed over the sun-bleached palm roofs of the town, and Rashid woke with a start, disoriented and a bit claustrophobic in his new surroundings. Despite the feeling of protection in the sheikh's walled home, he had suffered the same beginning since his last dawn in the desert. He wondered for a moment where Faisal and the silent traveler were greeting the day.

Feeling alone in the small house, he rose quietly and went to the doorway to see Mohammed slip through the gate like a shadow, carrying a heavy shapeless parcel. He stood listening for a while to the town slowly move into the life of morning, and jumped a bit as Fahad emerged through the gate in a hurry, notably disconcerted, and disappeared into the mews behind the house.

17.

Rashid managed his panic as he followed Mohammed and Fahad, weaving through a hot, bustling market. He focused his efforts on connecting with Mohammed to lighten the mood but was rewarded with surly or unresponsive glowers, so he left him alone. His uncle was more distant than the day before.

As they walked, he stopped among the bustle, flooded with the vague shadows of a memory of walking behind his father through a market on toddler legs and flashes of fear when he was separated from him. Lost in a strange sea of faces that seemed to know him, moving with the crowd past stalls of clinking, shimmering metals, music in perpetual celebration, unintentional mixes of oud and senseless riots of color and fragrance. A motherly hand had gripped his arm and pulled him from the river of sandals and robes to the small open curve of a vendor's tent, strangely awash with color. The face belonging to the hand was shrouded in a gold mask, the eyes behind it kind, knowing, and safe.

She sat wearily on a stool and whispered, "You're safe, *hayati*." She held out an amber piece of sweet *halwa* for him with a hand ornate with softly brown, faded henna scrolling. As he reached for it, she took his hand and looked at it for a moment, then studied his face as she wrapped his little hand around the sweet. He remembered the sticky taste of honey and cardamom as she stood and reached through the heavy oud smoke behind her, pulled folds of silk from a stack, and gently sorted through them. He watched wide-eyed, eating his sweet as she moved sapphire silk with single gold threads, emerald gold with squares of gold, solid, airy pieces the color of the moon. She watched his face glaze with fascination as one appeared and moved through the air like lighted ruby mercury, taking flight on its own by the lead of her hand. She gathered and stacked it like a gold necklace into one hand. Rashid was transfixed as she whispered something, reached into the wrap of silk now formed into the shape of a bird's nest, pulled out a misshapen pearl, and handed it to him, then pointed to the door, where his father stood, relieved and smiling.

    Fahad stood holding bundles of dates and provisions, looking at his strange nephew with concern. Rashid shook off the fog of memory and grabbed a few of the bundles to carry, then made a final thwarted friendly effort toward Mohammed as they walked toward Fahad's house.

    Much to Fahad's amusement, Mohammed glowered as Rashid expertly changed the haphazard mess Mohammed had created in his attempt to pack his camel, who was surly by habit and, it seemed to Rashid, by association. With balanced loads, the morning prayer faded through the city as they made their way through the thinning population of the town into the sunrise, where the masts of *dhows* began to appear over the sands. Rashid was spellbound as the sun caught them in the golden hour of morning. The horizon dropped as they continued, revealing the ocean. They rode along the coast, passing dhows being treated with shark oil, fishermen pulling in catches of needlefish, and more dhows arriving with fresh dates for market. Farther out were boats of pearl divers, readying to spend their days searching through cerulean water, lungs aching with the hope of opalescent treasures. Fahad watched them and studied Rashid's curiosity.

"When I left the desert for life in town, I went to the market for coffee and met a man who had made a fortune in the pearling industry. He always found them. The best," Fahad said with a smile. "His pearls were worn by the sheikh's family and transported to the royal families of Europe." Fahad watched the men dive from the distant boats. "By the end of our conversation, he had me convinced to become a diver for the pearling fleet…but God had other ideas."

"What happened?" asked Rashid, looking at him dry on his camel with a falcon on his arm.

"Two things," he said. "The pearl market crashed when the Japanese learned how to culture pearls and…" He smirked. "I sink like a stone, and they thought that was a valuable skill."

A smile cracked even Mohammed's face. Laughing at himself, Fahad looked at the Lanner falcon on his arm. "I suppose I was long determined to be part of what flies instead of what swims." He looked at Rashid and saddened. "I'm sorry I didn't know you before now, Rashid. Your father was my hero when we were young boys. He could swim…Your father could do anything."

As the distance grew between the falconers and town, Rashid became more comfortable, and his ease with his uncle and familiarity with the desert brought out a character he didn't realize he had. He found that his understanding of the desert, which he believed appeared challenged to some, seemed to surpass that of his city companions—even his uncle. For once in his life, he was the teacher, and he took careful pleasure in it. With his lessons, the humor of the caravan began to emerge, to the utter chagrin of Mohammed and the amusement of Fahad, who reveled deeply in this feeling of family.

The landscape changed as they traveled. As they entered the salt-pan region, they crossed an area where the rains had passed, and Fahad put Rashid to the test.

"Will we see migratory falcons here, Rashid?"

Rashid dismounted and dug into the sand to see how far the rain had penetrated. "It may be two or three months yet before the grass will grow here. Not before that."

Mohammed snorted in his skepticism, but Fahad looked at him with measured and growing respect.

"Good. That means the falcons will be hungry. Tomorrow we'll reach my place. A migratory funnel where they gather as they pass through while heading south." Fahad studied his nephew, deciding how much to teach him. Deciding how much to trust him. "Tell me why I would choose this place…"

Rashid felt the study and wanted to impress his uncle. "They love to exist at the edge of the season. Living on the edge is their way of honoring nature, and they must use the coastline and the peninsula head as a landmark to bring them all here. Like Abu Dhabi, it's cooler here and closer to rain and shorebirds for prey along the way, smarter for a falcon wishing for a safe journey instead of a solitary one."

Fahad smiled. "Where does a man of fifteen gain this knowledge?" he asked.

"He doesn't have knowledge. Only theory and hope. Knowledge belongs to God."

Fahad laughed out loud. Great rusty, rolling belly laughs. He ruffled Rashid's hair. "Your father was a wise goat too. Perhaps God will be good and offer a Saker falcon for us. If He does, with such a blessing, we'll be done. I can get married, and we can live like kings."

Somewhere during the mark of days as they traveled, they spotted the silhouette of a falcon circling on a thermal over the salt flats. Fahad stopped, they dismounted, and he sent Mohammed away with the camels. From a quickly dug blind covered with salt bushes, he tied a long line to a large shrike and released it. Rashid had seen falcons in the wild and recognized them, but they seemed to him as tangible as the wind. The falcon stooped to the bird, struck it, and bound to it. The falcon then flew a short distance and landed with the heavy bird rather than carrying it. Fahad, moving smoothly like water, made his way to the string without stirring the falcon. Slowly he pulled the kill away and walked back, leaving the dead bird fifty meters downwind from the blind, keeping the line tied to it in hand. Holding the line, he and Rashid waited.

"If God wills, he will return," Fahad said.

The falcon did return, gingerly clutching the shrike in its talons. Every time it started to feed, Fahad drew the line in, dragging the dead bird and falcon closer and closer. For a moment, the falcon fed only feet from the two hidden men. Rashid was in awe of the proximity of the wild bird. Like a cat, Fahad snapped out his hand and caught the falcon by the talons. "Shaheen!" he said proudly, announcing the Peregrine in his grasp with a grand smile before hooding and carrying the bird to Mohammed.

Rashid saw Mohammed smile for the first time. "God is good to us," Fahad said, meaning it.

The hooded Peregrine, lit by firelight, rested with another newly caught falcon on a square frame as Fahad and Mohammed made bread in the fire. Rashid couldn't tear his eyes away from the hooded bird. "I've never seen one this close," he whispered.

"That's true of women too, isn't it? That's about the way you looked at Salama," Fahad teased him.

"Salama? How did you see…I never looked at…"

Mohammed laughed cruelly. "Pfft. I have a better chance than you do at that one!"

Rashid ripped back, "I don't know about that. I don't smell so badly that dogs work to stay upwind of me, and unless she may have an affection for the face of a camel's backside, I'd say I have the better chance."

Fahad roared with laughter as the insults continued to fly, Rashid teasing, Mohammed teetering between genuine laughter and anger.

Rashid stirred long before dawn and found his uncle missing. The mongrel kept him company as he walked away from the camp and stood looking at the desert. Searching, perhaps. Fahad appeared from the night, startling Rashid. "He's still out there," Rashid said, nearly in a whisper.

"Makar Samūm? Yes. Yes, he is still out there, Rashid."

Rashid looked at him in the dark. "You believe me, don't you?"

Fahad looked at him sadly. And they stood in silence.

"My father said as he died not to avenge him. He said that a life spent in revenge was a life wasted."

Fahad recoiled a little, perhaps in anger. "He did, did he? Rashid, you need to decide who you are to become before you know the thing that will give you peace with it.

Your justice for what happened may only be found in your own truth."

"What about you, Uncle? He killed your brother. Aren't you angry?"

With a deep, thoughtful sigh, Fahad replied, "My brother was long dead to me until our sheikh told me he had been slain and until I met you. I had said goodbye to him long ago. My role in this is to prepare you, my only family, an innocent, for whatever you must do. I promise I will not fail you in that, so long as you don't fail your strength and truth." His voice lightened. "If we're clever and if you rise to it, perhaps we may somehow even convince our sheikh that you are the best man for his Salama in the process, and you'll too be the family of the royals."

Rashid smiled sheepishly, though the attachment hadn't occurred to him and found little anchor.

"They say her mother is Bedouin, you know." Fahad elbowed Rashid.

They stood in silence, waiting for the morning to come. There in the darkness, Fahad sighed with decision. "The sheikh will choose the birds he likes, but they are of far more value if they are trained." He thought for a moment. "The same may be said for you. So I will teach you everything I know about the art of falconry. Like all art, once you have the information, you must make it your own. Let me forewarn you: you cannot fake this. Our sheikh is one of the best falconers I know, with the keenest eye and finest instinct for it. Not only will he not buy birds with bad manners; he'll know something of the character of the man selling it. So you must do exactly what I do, which may differ from other falconers, and do exactly what I tell you." He paused and became grave. "You must also swear, by your father's honor, your oath to never reveal my methods to anyone but me, or your son." He looked hard at Rashid. "Yes or no?"

The mongrel looked toward the camp and wagged his tail.

"Mohammed, you too, I suppose. Yes or no?"

The eavesdropper trotted back to camp.

As the sun made its way to morning, it etched the silhouette of two lads sitting, steady, with hungry falcons on their arms. The first test of patience had begun. Rashid felt utterly at home with the weight of the Shaheen on his arm. It was as if that very weight had merely been missing and the instinct of movement to calm a falcon was a natural extension of him. The bird on his arm acquiesced quickly, bending to accept the morsel he held for her, and he rewarded her for it. He hooded her, let her rest, and readied for the next bird. Mohammed watched in jealousy as his chocolate-and-cream-colored Lanner bated again and again, his arm aching from the hours of holding her until she gave in. She refused. Fahad hooded her for him and gave him a break, to his embarrassment. Finally, as Rashid's second bird lowered her curved beak to the piece of meat he held and accepted it from him, Mohammed breathed deeply, and his Lanner seemed to do the same. She reached down and took the drying morsel, and he hooded the bird awkwardly in triumph.

18.

The training lads and falcons continued through the days, with bating, hooding, and the progress of building the furniture of jesses and new hoods. Mohammed's shine emerged in his artistry and perfection with making hoods and anklets and jesses. Even Fahad could find no fault in them, going as far as to admire and study them when the lads weren't looking. The progression continued, with the birds repeatedly flying to hand for food, first with leashes, then with a longer creance. Fahad taught them how to make a lure that would resemble a bustard, or small bird. Mohammed's looked like a master's sculpture of the beast itself, while Rashid's more closely resembled the mongrel who studied them sheepishly.

"Your day is here," Fahad said along the course of a morning that seemed otherwise like the rest. "Now we trust your foundations." Rashid's heart began to thump wildly. "Rashid, is she ready to fly?"

Rashid reached to the bird's chest and felt her keel, the point of her chest, to ascertain her weight and motivation to remain with him. "Yes."

Fahad touched her keel also but said nothing.

"All right..." Rashid removed the terrible first hood he had made for her, and she roused, straightening her feathers, and looked down at his glove for a morsel. Fahad nodded, prompting Rashid to remove the leash, leaving only her jesses in his hand. He held his breath, cast her off, and his face fell as he watched her lift from him and feel her freedom. With a shaky hand, he held a piece of meat in his raised hand, and his face nearly split in two with the strength of his grin as she faithfully flew to it and accepted her reward. Fahad knowingly mirrored his grin.

With help from Mohammed, Rashid's hoods began to take a shape that no longer resembled a camel's foot, and he returned the favor by helping to teach his mantling, hissing Lanner better manners. They found the tenuous beginnings of friendship.

As the careful securing of jesses and bells continued, Fahad's disapproval loosened, and they began learning the dance of flying a falcon to the lure. The young falconers were mesmerized, watching Fahad swing the lure, enticing the falcon to hunt with poetry in her movement and timing. She learned the game, to stalk and chase the lure with all the speed and coordination in her being, because she knew if she touched it, if she caught it, it meant a crop full of food. Even with falconer error, if she bested him, regardless of where they were in the day's training, it was a matter of honor and trust that she receive her reward. Fahad was perfect in his timing, speeding up the lure so it was only centimeters from her talons, which encouraged her to fight for it.

Mohammed's bird bound to the lure on the first swing, day after day. One such day, the twisted leather lead broke from the lure, and she ran with it, flapping and dragging it over a dune, with Mohammed running wildly to catch her, to the roaring laughter of Fahad. Finally she was fat and slow enough that she couldn't catch Mohammed's lure and had to work hard to turn her unfit self around to go back for a second dive, and a third. Finally he let her catch it and made in to her, both panting and gasping for air. They were a perfect match. For once Mohammed seemed pleased with himself and finally found a degree of kinship with Rashid as they walked back to the camp, carrying their falcons, filled with the satisfaction of the day.

Morning found Rashid's Peregrine stooping like a bullet to the lure, with Fahad watching in admiration. As the falconer, he rarely had an opportunity to simply witness the dance. Rashid had practiced and watched the lure, and this falcon responded to him as a flower to sunshine. In the beauty of such a sunrise, Fahad saw the shadow of his brother, and grief and anger joined joy. Rashid paused the lure, and in one gracious moment, the Peregrine hit it, bound to it, and Rashid swept it gently to the ground. He made in to the bird, and she hopped lightly to his cuff to trade her catch for a reward. He walked to his uncle with a grin and watched him shift his layers of emotion into a simple, clear smile. "Are you sure your father never taught you falconry?"

Rashid shrugged. "My father wasn't a falconer. He never had a bird."

Fahad studied him with a sense of disbelief for an instant before shifting his reaction to a smirk. "Well then, it must be because you're related to me! You have a true gift with this, Rashid, which makes more sense than you know. It comes from your heart. Perhaps one day God will be good to us and bring a Saker falcon across our path. That is nearly as good as nobility."

Mohammed stopped as they walked toward him into camp. The outsider. He turned quickly away.

"Mohammed!" Fahad called with good nature. "Are you going to fly your bird or just rest in camp today?"

Mohammed stopped and turned around self-consciously, holding a handful of leather. Fahad and Rashid looked to the edge of the camp, where the falcons they had trapped were quietly perched and tethered perfectly in a row.

"My falconers," Fahad said with a satisfied grin, "I believe we are ready."

19.

The desert wind gently blew the fine fabric of Rashid's new white robes as he stepped beside a catch with the three Peregrines. Mohammed stood nervously with another frame where three hooded Lanner falcons rested easily. Fahad emerged from a fine tent between them and scanned the skyline. He looked at Mohammed and took in his nervousness. "What is it? Worried about meeting the sheikh? Not to worry. Rashid here is his new friend."

Mohammed looked down. Fahad followed his gaze, and his face shifted. Before each bird was a perfect new goat-leather hood with careful etched scrolling adorning the sides, leather jesses with matching scrolling, and a braided goat-leather leash. In front of the perch for Rashid's Peregrine was one with complete perfect scrolling. Fahad and Rashid were speechless.

"How did…" Fahad didn't know what to ask.

"I traded for the leather at market…I thought the sheikh shouldn't have field furniture on his falcons."

"Well!" Fahad boomed, glowering, insulted. Mohammed stood wide-eyed for a moment before Fahad clapped him on the shoulder.

20.

Fahad broke into a huge smile as his nervousness turned to fierce, hungry admiration, and he gestured to Rashid to the dune in front of them. Over the crest of the dune appeared a line of riders on horses, crisp against the sky. The sheikh appeared, surrounded by his guards, sons, daughters, nephews, and nieces. He was the proud and gentle nucleus of his world and took the lead as the line poured down the face of the dune, the ornamented horses fresh in their task. Rashid searched for Salama and found her among her cousins, riding the unmistakable, enormous, ethereal Malaak near the back of the group. The sheikh drew up to a halt dramatically and dismounted, and as he clapped the shoulder of one of his sons standing next to Saif, Rashid looked down, missing his father.

The sadness wasn't lost on the sheikh. "Word has reached me that our Rashid here is quite the master at this. His work may help him become family as well, ay, Fahad?" He greeted Fahad warmly as he approached and looked carefully at the Peregrines. "Show us your work then, young man! Let's see if you have tipped the scales to pay your uncle's dowry."

Rashid looked at his friend Saif, who smirked at him and nodded him on, then stepped into his moment by placing one of the Peregrines on the sheikh's cuff and taking his own to hunt. As they walked past the tent, Rashid caught a glimpse of Salama watching him with admiration. With effort, she looked away, pretending to be mysterious and busy with her horse. The sheikh saw the exchange and looked with a question at Fahad, who shrugged knowingly.

Falcons cast and stooped to the familiar awe of the party flying them, and the sheikh's admiration mirrored Fahad's pride at the reaction to his birds and to his nephew, who was putting on a show for them, taking turns with his uncle explaining the quality of each bird. Sadness washed over Fahad for a moment as he recognized his brother in Rashid. The Peregrines flew and hunted with prowess and exacting partnership with him. The mongrel dog sat dutifully beside the tent, watching them, as Mohammed's chubby Lanner pumped her wings as hard as she could to capture the lure. On her third attempt, she bound to it and fell with a thump to the sand. Laughter rolled through the group. As Mohammed approached, she mantled and hissed and tried to drag the lure. His face flushed scarlet. As Rashid made in to pick her up, she bobbed her head and took off. The mongrel left Rashid for the first time to run after the falcon over a rise. The group followed.

"Did you train this one then?" the sheikh asked as they ran.

"Your Highness," said Rashid, "perhaps God gives us one to keep us wise and humble."

Fahad's anger and embarrassment rose through him as they made their way to the rise. The mongrel barked brightly, which seemed a further insult to the moment.

The sheikh crested the rise with Rashid before Fahad and the others, and the sheikh began booming with excitement. "Look!" The Lanner was bound to a houbara far larger than she and was fighting it with the entirety of her being. Mohammed stopped in his tracks, as they all did, to watch the spectacle. No part of the houbara's fight or struggle would extricate it from her determined grip, and together they bucked and rolled and beat their wings against each other. Finally she pinned down the fierce prey's head, and in a frenzied flurry, her tomial tooth found its place, and she spun it with the full force of her body, killing her overworthy prey.

They all stood motionless and silent as she panted, her talons around the beak and neck of her prey, her spiked beak still buried. She raised her head, and her feathers smoothed flat against her body, save for those broken by the mighty houbara, and she waited for them like a little queen, unmoving even as they roared into a cheer, still not believing what they had seen. The sheikh, booming with laughter, slapped Rashid on the back.

"That's Mohammed's bird," Rashid said with a smile, but the sheikh didn't hear him as he himself made in to the Lanner, offered a piece of liver in trade for her prize, and scooped her up with ceremony and fed her to her heart's content, the whole time laughing in admiration.

"She isn't a Saker. But this may be my favorite bird you have ever brought me! Well done, Fahad! Well done, Rashid, my son!" Laughing, he walked on toward the tents.

Rashid looked to Fahad to rectify the confusion, but Fahad shook his head slightly. Saif understood but, in a look, concurred with Fahad. Now wasn't the time. Mohammed sunk into a black glower as they walked, glaring daggers at Rashid.

They rounded the edge of the tent with falcons in hand and the sheikh laughing. He saw Salama gazing at Rashid, shook his head, and clapped Rashid on the shoulder in the same manner he had his son. "Fahad! How much do you need for my greedy brother-in-law's dowry? You should be close by now with this outstanding group."

Fahad smiled discreetly.

"Close enough to set plans in motion. I'll honor your promise in trust. You will marry my niece one month from today. Right here in this place! You may deliver all the birds, Fahad. I'll buy them all." He looked directly at the groom. "In fact, I'll honor your *entire* dowry if you can manage to get just one Saker falcon for me, trained by the bravest of your two lads."

Fahad looked at the two boys and studied them to gauge their understanding of the challenge just thrown down for them.

21.

The elaborate tents shone warmly as circles of fires and lanterns were lit to warm against the last light of day fading across the dunes. As they approached the entrance of the sheikh's tent, Rashid quickly scanned for Salama, wondering as always if she was a dream. Mohammed looked at the stone-faced guard with grave intimidation, and Rashid paused, unsure how to proceed. In a fit of movement, the tent opened, and Saif burst out with a great light grin and greeted his old travel companion with the deep warmth of a brother. "You're not going to believe what they're going to have you do! It's a good thing you have me!"

The two young falconers looked at him in confusion. Trepidation crept across Mohammed's face, joining the glower still stamped there as they followed Saif into the tent, where the sheikh greeted them warmly, proudly. Fahad was already seated in the cushions with an ornate silver cup for tea in his hand. Completely self-possessed, he was profoundly content in the lush surroundings. He looked at the two young men with pride and a greedy glint that they represented him so very well, furthering his comfort in that place. They shyly accepted dates and coffee and followed Saif closely, grateful for the lead.

As they settled into a corner, the sheikh spoke with a twinkle. "Which one of you lads is the bravest?"

Mohammed jumped up, narrowing his eyes at Rashid. A ripple of appreciative laughter moved through the tent.

"Do you ride, young falconer?" the sheikh asked Mohammed. "Horses."

Mohammed's eyes grew round. Out of his disdain for horses, he had developed an allergy to them. He shook his head.

The sheikh smiled. "Well, now is your chance. You are going to help me settle a long-standing question. There are two horses ridden by my children; both are reported to be the strongest and fastest. One is a better rider than the other, so I must settle the question of their quality another way. Tomorrow there will be a race. As you are the bravest, young falconer, you may choose your horse first."

Saif walked to Mohammed with two large tassels, one deep blue, the other red. As Mohammed studied them, Saif looked at him, looked hard at the red, and wagged it almost imperceptibly. Mohammed studied him, glared at Rashid, and chose the blue. As he handed the red tassel to Rashid, Saif winked.

"Mohammed, you will be riding my Asjan. Rashid, you will be riding Malaak...God help you. Someone got the name wrong with that one. 'Angel...'" he muttered, shaking his head. "The others have already chosen. Tomorrow you'll have one minute to speak with their normal riders for instructions...Then I will give you the quest for your ride." Rashid was hit with a jolt of nerves. He would get to talk to her.

Fahad walked them back to the tent, and they stopped to check on the falcons. As they looked over the resting birds, he said, "You two have given me honor. I'm grateful."

"I won't be with you much longer, sir," said Mohammed. "I'm going to win that race and work for the sheikh."

"Well, you have the training for it, my lad." He picked up the Lanner and removed her hood. "He will call on you as a leather worker alone, judging from these. How on earth did you get this kind of leather?"

Mohammed kicked the ground shyly. "I made a deal with a traveler at market. I traded some old extra blankets and things I found in the mews at home."

Fahad's forehead furrowed for a moment. "Camel blankets?"

Mohammed shrugged. Fahad studied him.

"Well, good trading. I don't recall them." He replaced the hood on the small brown falcon and set her quietly on her perch. "We should go. You boys have a long day tomorrow!"

22.

Salama walked with her glaring maid on one side and Saif on the other as she led her horse toward Rashid. Her anger that he would ride him in such a race was wrapped in her otherwise aloof, monotone greeting. Saif nodded to her in exasperation, requesting her help for his friend. She sighed and then rounded on Rashid. "He knows more than you do. Tell him to go home and trust that he knows. Let him find his way through the dunes; he already knows where the footing is best. If you're lost, do not tell him where to go. He knows where to go. If the sand becomes too deep, don't be lazy. Get off him and walk. He can get you through it, and he'll be loyal if you respect him."

Rashid wasn't sure he had heard what she said for listening to her voice.

"Stay light on him. He moves like water; move with him. He will speak to you. Like all things, if you respect him and listen to him instead of yourself, he will show you all ways and will die for you if he must. You will feel it. If he dies for you, know that you are *not* worthy of him…or of anything else. I know him. If he loses, I'll know it's because you didn't earn his respect, and it will say something about you."

"Thank you," he croaked.

"Stay off his mouth, or you'll have to answer to me." She handed the soft red-tasseled reins to him, and Malaak watched her walk away in a cloud of silks. He looked taken aback and nickered at her. He looked at Rashid slowly from head to toe, sizing him up.

Salama turned back. "One more thing." She handed Rashid a woven red sash with a single pearl sewn into it. "You're not riding for your greedy uncle this time. Now you're riding for your sheikh."

His heart skipped a beat as she handed it to him, ran her hand down Malaak's neck and shoulder, and walked away. Saif rolled his eyes and shook his head carefully.

As Saif gave him a leg up, Rashid worked to appear less awkward than he was. Malaak was larger and felt more solid than Masroor. He also belonged to himself and cranked his ears suspiciously at this new rider, giving Rashid a clear message of the level of consequence he was capable of delivering.

"You're going to need to breathe at some point," Saif said, trying to be helpful.

The sheikh spoke. "As you are young men of the desert, your task is quite simple. On the way here, my favorite lantern fell from a camel. The one to bring it back to me will receive a reward, my favor, and an invitation to stay at my home and train for me."

Rashid looked at Mohammed, perched uncomfortably on his chestnut and glaring in hungry determination as one of Saif's brothers coached him, pointing in the direction of the tracks they had made riding to camp the day before and to the sun.

"Directions would be good," Rashid said nervously to Saif.

"Wouldn't do any good. I've seen your skills. Just follow the tracks. Follow him and his horse; Asjan will take him toward the palace and home for her. Let Malaak bring you back here. He will always come back to wherever my cousin is. She is home to him."

Rashid thought about that for a moment but kept it to himself that such an instinct made complete sense to him.

"You good?" said Saif.

"How do I make the saddle not hurt?"

"Don't ride…" Saif grinned at him.

As they rode from the tents, the rhythm was jarring and awkward. Mohammed and Asjan flew over the top of a dune and disappeared. Rashid didn't even try to tell Malaak where to go as he struggled and painfully failed to find the center of the ride, grasping for stability with the grand platinum mane. Malaak responded to the unbalanced flopping on his back with pinned ears as he snaked himself between dunes at a trot that banged Rashid's teeth. He refused to walk. Rashid clenched every muscle he had, fighting to find and change the movement and not fall off. He refused to canter. After a few minutes, Malaak stopped in his tracks and craned his head around to touch Rashid's foot and look back in the direction of the camp.

"Forgive me, Malaak," he said in agony. "This is less fun for me than it is for you, my friend. Can you help us out here?" Rashid caught his breath and squeezed his calves, and Malaak walked on slowly, allowing him to gather himself.

Saif's instructions returned. "Sit back. Drop your feet toward the earth. They're like camels, but scarcely touch the ground."

"He moves like water…" As Salama's words pushed everything else out of his mind, Malaak turned toward a dune to illustrate them. His efforts in the sand were heavier, but every movement softened together in the effort, and Rashid found that he was able to sit so it helped him. As they skated down the far side of the dune, Rashid let go, and everything softened to a flow, and the desert moved together with them. As they reached the bottom, Malaak lilted into a soft earth-covering canter. In it Rashid began to feel the story of the horse, his character connecting with an understanding of his own with Salama, and with the desert, and at once he understood the movement as being precisely what she had said, like water.

Al Rabea had always been much too noble and responsible to go past the occasional elegant trot, so Rashid had never flown over the desert like this. The ground sailed beneath them as the three hoofbeats seemed only to serve their easy flight. At such a speed, Malaak created his own wind for him, and in a moment, he understood something of a sense of being outside of himself that he hadn't before. He laughed out loud, and Malaak responded with a few beats of a true gallop as his welcome before settling back into an easy ground-covering gait. Asjan was nowhere in sight, but they occasionally crossed the tracks made by the sheikh and his family.

They rounded the edge of a dune, and a movement caught Rashid's eye. Malaak loosed a deep, roaring whinny. Asjan crested a dune, running crazily, riderless, with the prize, the sheikh's lantern tied to her saddle and bumping behind her. Rashid scanned the horizon from where she'd come and went numb and cold in a flash. In the distance, a small white figure lay motionless, another standing over him marked with deep red over his head.

    By the time Makar Samūm heard Malaak's whinny, Rashid had kicked the horse into a gallop over the swell and into the crevasse between dunes in a white fury toward his father's murderer and Mohammed. They emerged from the cleft between dunes and nearly ran over three tiny antelope bolting from a small brush. Malaak leaped away to avoid running into them, and the movement unseated Rashid. He hit the ground hard, a bolt of pain flashing through his head and shoulder, and every molecule of air rushed from his lungs. He struggled furiously in a shock of partial awareness toward Mohammed and Makar Samūm as his existence ached in a panic for breath. As the blur of consciousness faded, buzzing from the edges of his vision, he saw blue sky, white, and a flash of red.

23.

A moment passed. Perhaps it was a moment. He saw his father standing quietly in the fold of his unconsciousness, and relief swept over him. He felt safe. The silver flash of a falcon obscured the image and shook him into a struggle for consciousness as oxygen returned through the blur. The silver flash took the form of Malaak, who stood over him, nervous but motionless, save for Salama's red sash caught in the saddle, fluttering softly.

Rashid stood slowly, unsteadily, still pulling air back into his lungs, and leaned on Malaak as he struggled toward Mohammed.

He crawled to the edge of a rise and saw Mohammed alone and unmoving. He searched as far as he could in the direction of the tracks and saw nothing. Makar Samūm had disappeared.

Mohammed's chest and shoulder were soaked in blood, and there was a gash on his face. Rashid touched him, wondering if he was still alive, and he stirred and slowly wrenched his eyes open.

"Rashid." It was a whisper.

"What happened? What did you see?" asked Rashid.

Mohammed grimaced in pain and touched his shoulder. Rashid pulled back his robes to reveal the gape of a gunshot wound, and his breath caught.

"Did you do this to me?" Mohammed asked weakly.

Rashid stared hard, thinking. "Did you see his face?" Rashid asked. "Mohammed, did you see his face?" Mohammed slipped away from consciousness.

"Tell them it was me, Mohammed. Whomever finds you, tell them I did this."

24.

Rashid wasn't sure whether he heard him.

Malaak stood like a white stone as Rashid struggled and managed to get Mohammed up into the saddle and held him from the ground. "Take us to your girl," he said to Malaak, and the silver horse walked quickly toward the camp with Mohammed's blood falling down his shoulder, Rashid hurrying beside him.

The shadows lengthened as they moved with an agonizing speed of travel that would be caught by night. Rashid wondered if Malaak knew the danger this night would bring if they didn't make it back to the camp before sunset. He gave the horse the last of his water, and they moved on.

As indigo crept from the base of the dunes, bringing night with it, Malaak stopped and stiffened. His head shot up and his ears locked. He blew a roaring blast of air through his nose in alarm but did not whinny. He moved nervously, stopped when Mohammed was unbalanced, and blew again. Rashid, heart pounding, saw nothing, so he tugged at Malaak's bridle in an attempt to get him down into a depression and out of sight. Malaak grew roots, standing unmovable. Mohammed slid from the saddle, and Rashid, unable to reposition him, eased him to the ground and looked for something, anything, to cover him, hide him. Finding nothing, he stood, searching for the red guttrah to face what was coming.

Over a rise, the glint of three lanterns appeared, and Malaak blasted a roaring whinny. The lanterns moved toward them.

"Rashid!" the sheikh's voice carried over the distance. Malaak rumbled again, and the last of Rashid's adrenaline left him. "Over here," he could only whisper.

The lighted outlines of the sheikh, Fahad, and two of the sheikh's guards appeared on horseback in the advancing night. The sheikh and Fahad jumped from their horses and ran to Mohammed.

Mohammed stirred as they investigated the wound through his shoulder.

"What happened? Who did this? Did you see who did this?" asked Fahad.

Mohammed weakly raised his uninjured arm and pointed at Rashid. Fahad stared at him, then looked to the sheikh, and they both looked hard at Rashid.

"He had the lantern. He was going to win," said Rashid.

Fahad's face went white.

"Fahad, go. Get him to camp as fast as you can. My doctor is there. I'll bring Rashid with me," the sheikh said.

Fahad hesitated for a moment but knew he couldn't question his sheikh. He stared hard at Rashid, who bent his head for disappointing his uncle. He suddenly felt empty and alone with Fahad's departure.

With a mostly unconscious Mohammed up in the saddle in front of him, Fahad swung his horse around to stare through Rashid with an expression too dark and confused for Rashid to define. He said nothing and turned to ride fast out of the light toward the camp, with one of the guards in tow.

Rashid stepped into Malaak's saddle with more grace than before. The sheikh studied him

"Do you want to tell me what really happened?" the sheikh asked lightly, glancing at the blood on Malaak's left shoulder.

"It was as Mohammed said, Your Highness...He had the lantern, and was going to win so... it, it was me."

The sheikh nodded and asked his guard to ride ahead to check the trail.

"I wonder, Rashid," said the sheikh slowly once out of earshot of his guard, "where your rifle is..."

Rashid glanced down. His rifle was in his tent. It was only supposed to be a ride in safe quarter. Rashid looked at the face etched in wisdom, certain he knew the only plausible story and found himself ashamed that he had been caught in a lie by his sheikh.

"Swear to me your truth to this question, Rashid."

"I swear, sir."

"What did you see?"

"I saw Asjan running and Mohammed on the ground, unconscious. Makar Samūm was walking toward him but stopped at Malaak's whinny. I raced toward them, but Malaak spooked at some antelope and I fell off." The sheikh was silent for a long time.

"God sent this antelope to protect you, Rashid, didn't he? Do you know if he saw you?"

"I believe he saw someone. There is no way he could know who he was seeing."

"Did you see his face?" The sheikh was looking unblinkingly at him.

"No. I only saw red."

"Swear on your father."

"I swear it. I did not see his face." He blackened. "I wish I had."

They rode on through the advance of night in silence.

"To protect you, from Makar Samūm, I will have to punish you to keep appearances." the sheikh said slowly.

Rashid nodded.

"You will have to trust your abilities, Rashid, and you must stay true to your story and tell no one anything else. Do you understand? Not Saif, not your uncle, no one."

Rashid suddenly felt alone, and a glint arose that he could now truly trust no one. He slowly studied the man who rode beside him. "God will show us through this," he said.

"Yes. God is good," said the sheikh.

25.

They arrived back at the camp, and Rashid wondered if it was his imagination that it had had a joyful, celebratory center of life and light only that morning. A heavy fearful pall hung over it as they rode in, and all eyes, without being seen, studied the boy with the sheikh and the blood on Malaak's shoulder. Rashid could feel it and ached to flee from it. They rode past the tent with the falcons, and he wondered if he would ever get to fly them again.

They dismounted, and Rashid watched as a groom led Malaak away. The great white horse stopped and craned his head around to study Rashid for a moment, flipped his tail, and walked on with the groom. The sheikh studied him long and hard. "Go see to your falcons and then directly to your tent. I will send for you in the morning." He spoke quietly with his guard and sent Rashid with him.

He stepped into the tent where the falcons rested quietly on their perches wearing Mohammed's beautiful jesses and hoods. Rashid quietly picked up Mohammed's Lanner, who rested on his cuff still proud of her feat. He stroked her chest feathers quietly and with a heavy heart, placed her on her perch and made his way to his uncle.

The mongrel wagged his tail at Rashid, and Fahad emerged from their tent as he and the guard approached. His face twisted when he saw his nephew.

"I'm sorry, Uncle." Rashid felt an old familiar stab of shame, of the disappointment he had caused his father.

"Do you know the penalty for this, Rashid? If Mohammed dies, the sheikh will put you to death." He said, frowning at his nephew. "What are you not telling me?" Fahad's tone had gone black. "Rashid, I am your family. You can tell me."

Rashid looked down, shredded with an agony of indecision. The guard shifted at the opening of the tent. He could hear everything.

"I'm sorry, Uncle..." he repeated, trying to fill the space and find the answer to what he should say.

Fahad saw him glance at the guard. Perhaps understanding, he disengaged in anger. Rashid, exhausted, fell into a heap.

The flaps of their tent flew open before dawn.

"Fahad," the guard said from the dark, waking them. As Fahad rose to join him outside, the guard rumbled again. "You too." They followed him to the falcon tent, where the entrance was torn and haphazardly open. The sheikh himself stood by the door.

"You need to see this." The sheikh's voice was quiet and dark.

They walked in with lanterns to see a single falcon left, unhooded and bating frantically, tethered by only one jess. The rest of the place had been ransacked. Rashid was distraught as he sank to the perch where his own Peregrine had been, now marked only with slashed jesses, Mohammed's hood, and a few feathers remaining to prove she had once been there. All the rest of the falcons, including Mohammed's proud Lanner, were gone.

Fahad snapped and rounded on Rashid in a rage.

"You. You have failed me, you have ruined yourself, and now you have ruined me as well," he snarled. "You are no better than your father."

A guard appeared and whispered to the sheikh. In a breath, he summoned his kinship with hundreds of years of leadership to cloak his natural reaction. "Mohammed has died. He lost too much blood."

Fahad's face turned to stone, and he looked at the ground.

The tent began to spin around Rashid.

"Rashid." The sheikh's tone brought him back. "Go to your tent. I will deal with you there. Fahad, come with me. I must speak with you."

Rashid's uncle stared through him as he was pulled through the entrance and walked in the grip of the guard to his tent.

He sat alone, reeling.

26.

"Rashid."

The blood roaring in his ears seemed to take shape. Had the desert said something?

"Rashid, come here quickly." breathed the whisper again, sounding from the back of the tent. The corner had been opened to the night. Salama stood there in the night, holding his satchel and rifle. "Do not whisper a word. You must leave right now while they're distracted with the falcons. Everything is in here." She pulled him through the opening and shoved his rifle and satchel into his hands. "Go. Now. Quickly."

He stared at her for a moment in amazement as she shoved sadness out of her eyes. He mouthed a silent thank-you, and ran from the encampment.

The mongrel appeared, trotting to the falcon-tent entrance with a dead falcon in his mouth. He dropped it gently at the sheikh's feet and looked in the direction of Rashid's tent. Fahad drew his gun and aimed at the dog. Just as he was about to pull the trigger, the sheikh pushed it away. He picked up the dead Peregrine and inspected it. Her neck had been broken.

"Let there be no more injustice this morning." He said quietly. "That beast didn't kill this falcon."

The mongrel took off at a sprint and ran into the dark. From the shadows, Salama watched him go after Rashid and blessed him.

27.

The desert might have thought Rashid was a little bigger than he had been before as he walked accompanied only by the mongrel, who he tried to no avail to chase away. The temperament of landscape changed around him nearly without his notice as he walked, deep in thought, wondering and questioning what he had missed, working through his confusion at his situation. Had he been so deep in thought that he left the falcon tent open? He held his rifle steady with a rabbit in his sights and pulled the trigger. Sitting next to a small fire as the sun disappeared, he looked hard at the dog, made a decision, and handed the mongrel a piece of the rabbit. He reached into his satchel, pulled out Salama's woven sash, and ran his hand over it sadly. His thumb found a lump, and he searched the sash to reveal the pearl she had woven into it. In a moment, the masked lady in the market emerged in his memory, and her whisper rose through time.

"Know what you want to find, and God will show it to you if you have wisdom."

He knew his answer.

"Looks like we will have to do it ourselves."

The mongrel's head tilted.

Lying in watch next to Rashid, the dog seemed to understand the game. They waited low and motionless together as another shrike wandered into Rashid's snare. In one movement, he caught the bird, and as he swept it into his pouch, the mongrel whined, looking up. Rashid squinted to the sky but saw nothing. He shook his head, shouldered his rifle, and walked away. The dog sat, watching the sky.

Rashid figured the mongrel would change his mind once he rounded a rise and lost sight of him. Not so. He continued to walk. Finally, from the distance, he heard a plaintive, high-pitched yip. Still the dog didn't come. With a sigh, he looked up again. From the blue moved something nearly imperceptible; a wisp of cloud perhaps, he thought. He caught the movement again and watched hard for it to take shape but lost its place in the enormous empty cobalt sky. He walked back around the rise to see the dog still sitting, still looking up, tilting his head. Rashid walked back to him, stumbling as he scanned the sky. A speck of cloud streaked across the blue, caught sun, drew wings, and took the shape of the tiny silhouette of a falcon deep in the distance. As they watched, the bird turned and slid into a stoop with the same bravery as his beloved Peregrine. As shadow and shape fused into form and detail, Rashid's breath caught in amazement.

"It's enormous! What is it? My God. That's... that's a Saker, isn't it?" He watched in disbelief. It was a Saker falcon...but white as the cloud from which it had appeared. The dog's tail wagged. "You're right. God is good to us." They watched as the falcon dove and turned, elegantly wrapping around a fleeing bird and disappearing over a rise as she took it to ground. Rashid ran low with stealth, flattened himself against the small rise, and inched himself to the edge. He peeked over the crest to see a nearly pure-white falcon stain the feathers of her beautiful face red as she tore delicately into her prey. Rashid watched in disbelief and backed away, trembling with excitement. He reached into his satchel and pulled out the remains of Mohammed's beautiful hood and jesses as well as some scraps of leather and wax. He looked at them and then back at the bird. The dog, lying flat next to him, wagged his tail.

    For days he hid in a blind, released shrikes, and watched the falcon hunt them as he refashioned the hood and jesses from the leather, smiling as he threaded the pearl and red yarns from the tassel of Salama's weaving as the top knot and plume. Even Mohammed would have been impressed. Behind and above him, the falcon tilted with the afternoon. Rashid watched her, transfixed.

    The desert passed easily beneath her, the changing waves and shapes already anchored maps in her very creation. This place in the ocean of desert had been good to her, but she was hungry. A movement caught her. A shrike hopped haphazardly along the sand. The small bird seemed injured, so the falcon flattened and flew low, stalking. She tilted and rose into the sun, then folded her white wings to her body and dove. She approached the shrike and, inexplicably, missed it. Perplexed, she turned hard and returned to hit it again, moving like light itself toward her prey. She struck it, and instantly it was dead. She landed and hopped sideways toward her breakfast, then stopped. Something had made her nervous. She looked around in slow silence, a soft breeze rolling a few loose feathers from her prey and the movement overthrew her caution. She reached to take the bird, and the red sand around her came alive in a single fluid movement.

    From the movement, the hand of the desert caught her talons and stood. The flapping of her ethereal wings against Rashid's outstretched arm created a storm, pushing the sand like a summer squall from his white tunic as he held her high to protect her feathers. In his other hand, he still held the shrike where she could see it. The hood materialized, and before she was aware of it, he slipped it over her head. Immediately she calmed and searched, disoriented, for her balance. With one hand and a movement old despite his years, Rashid slid jesses around her delicate pale tarsus, then slowly stilled himself, and waited.

With the great white bird on his fist and the mongrel lying calmly beside him, Rashid, without moving, watched the desert ease into evening and missed his father. In the dimming light of dusk, he slowly reached up and removed her hood. Her beak opened, and she hissed and panted, her wings up. She bated, diving from his fist, held fast, to her surprise, by the jesses. In a movement originated by her, he helped her gracefully back to his fist, where she stood panting, deciding whether she still had her dignity. To her dismay, he quietly offered her a piece of meat, holding it calmly near her talons, and he waited.

28.

Evening became night, and they waited. Dawn washed over the tiring trio, and they sat still as the rising sun, Rashid shifting only to replace his offering for a fresh piece. Through the day, they sat together, and Rashid fought hard against the savage onslaught of sleep. The falcon's white feathers were the same as the robes of his father. The red meat, the ghutrah of Makar Samūm. Somewhere behind his father's robes, the afternoon desert stirred in a breeze that whispered into his father's voice, singing the evening prayer, and the white robes moved rousing him from his delirium as the great white falcon changed her posture and looked straight into Rashid, seeing his ancestors. As time stood still, she looked with eyes the color of his father's coffee, of Salama's eyes, of the white oryx, of his own. Slowly she stretched her elegant white head down and took the food from his fingers. She was with him. He allowed her to eat, then placed the hood on her.

    At sunrise, Rashid rose, prayed, and slung his satchel over his shoulder. He picked up the falcon and walked stiffly into the desert, the mongrel stepping in tow. Walking with the falcon on his fist felt strangely natural, although the weight of her was something new, and his muscles ached. He thought of Salama and wondered whether she was riding her horse among her cousins, making her way back to the garden behind the walls, or still in the desert where she was so free and at ease. He ached at the thought of her. He scanned the horizon as he walked, heavy with the thought. She had helped him.

Rashid remembered his father's expression as he had scanned the horizon while they walked. He adopted it as he walked along, carrying the falcon and understanding something of being a guardian. During one of these sweeps, he spotted a camel train moving slowly across a near horizon. He lifted his light water skin and changed direction to make his way toward it. The camels slowed as they saw him. He dropped a handful of sand in peace, and they did the same, waving him over. He approached them carefully as their faces were obscured, wrapped in protective head- and face gear. They waited for a moment, then lowered the white cloths to reveal smiling faces. Rashid was overjoyed to find the familiar faces of his friends among them. Faisal walked to him with his hand extended, put his forehead warmly to Rashid's. What were the chances?

"Yes! So, Xunfasaa!" he laughed warmly to Rashid, "but can you shoot?" There were new travelers with his old caravan, but those whom he knew greeted him one by one like brothers.

"Your story gets better every time we see you, young Rashid! What are the chances that we would find you alone out here again?" The spectacled traveler coughed and cleared his throat to cover his emotion.

"I'm not alone, my friend," Rashid replied a little proudly.

"Yes, it would seem God has been good to you to give you such guardians! Are they an improvement from us?" they teased him.

"That's a high price someone paid you not to trade your rifle," another chimed in. Faisal decided that was where they would stop to camp and called them to make coffee.

Rashid handed him a date. Faisal smiled at the new wiser face of this young man.

As they settled into the efficiency and habit of movement, unraveling the loads into the constant geometry of camp for another evening of rest, the Silent Tribesman appeared where the fire would be and stopped in shock when he saw the falcon. His eyes grew round, and he lost himself in it for a moment, unable to pull himself from her gaze or gather his composure. He was nearly beside himself, dumbstruck, with an expression like that of a lover lost then found again in another lifetime. He pulled his gaze to Rashid and slowly shifted to recognition and a shocked realization. Rashid felt eyes on him, looked at the Silent Tribesman, and grinned. The elegant man regained his composure with effort and joined the gathering group in his customary place.

With the peace of coffee, the men goaded Rashid into telling his story. There were new faces among them, of course, but as Rashid spoke, those who knew him noted the change in the quiet, traumatized lad they had taken in on their previous journey. He told them of his uncle and the falconry and the dowry, and bravely, he told them about his mistake that might have led to the ruin of his uncle's chances. He left out Makar Samūm.

"God is good," he said, looking at the falcon resting next to him on a perch he had fashioned. "She will make things right with my uncle and with the sheikh before the wedding."

"When is that?" Faisal questioned. "Our sheikh likes weddings on full moons."

Rashid nodded at him.

"If that's true, you have less than a week to get there." Faisal looked at him gravely. "It isn't safe for you to be out here alone with Makar Samūm out there."

The other familiar faces around the circle nodded and mumbled with one another, expressing their concern for him and his safety; after all, he had never failed in killing every person who had laid eyes on him, and surely by now word had reached him that he had been seen when he killed Rashid's father. A young man new to the caravan chimed in with a grisly tale of the mythic outlaw, topped by another legend poem, ending with the statement that most believed he wasn't really a man but the gathering of an evil black omen that foretold the death of any being it saw. Rashid's friends winced and looked to him for a response. He gave none.

"I don't believe it," said the spectacled traveler broke the embarrassment, "but what could possibly happen to make a man become so evil?"

"Betrayal. Greed and significance."

They all stopped in mid gesture and looked at the Silent Tribesman in disbelief as he spoke. Most present had never heard his voice.

"A dangerous combination."

They moved slowly, as they would in front of a bird they didn't want to fly away or a snake they didn't want to provoke to strike.

"They say," he said in the slow, mocking inflection that normally accompanied stories begun about the criminal, "he is the last son of an ancient tribe of mythical warriors. Most believe this tribe is no more than a story to connect children with their desert ancestors."

The travelers settled down as he decided whether to continue. He glanced at Rashid, and his face grew distant as he searched the coals beneath the arched coffeepot.

"They were first revered as great hunters, saving entire families and tribes of fellow Bedouin people with successful hunts during droughts and famine. No one knew how. It seemed the desert spoke to them when their intentions were noble, which they always were. Their skills together made them coveted and secretive, warriors and mercenaries for honorable causes. The legend of their fearsome skills was so well known, it was said they were called in secret to defend Petra, where they were heralded for holding off Antigonus I Monophthalmus, the brutal young general to Alexander the Great himself, as well as Roman invaders hungry for the trade route through Petra. Though they never claimed it, they were said in whispers to be protected a thousand years ago by Al Qiyam, a distant Nabataean god of war and the night and protector of caravans, and they were exceptionally well educated.

"With such legend comes a price. They were celebrated, yes, but they were also feared. They became the test of bravery for entire tribes that attacked them for notoriety and, without exception, perished at their hand, so protecting their secret. There was a bounty on their belongings and by proof of any of them killed. The price of their greatness. So they went into seclusion, living secretly, peacefully, as peasants among nomads and city dwellers while keeping their story silent for nearly fifty generations. Nothing changed, nothing grew, and their legend slept in obscurity. The legend was that twice in a generation, the families of the great tribe gathered to pass along their traditions and their secret to those among them who were most worthy of it. If there were none worthy, the generation was left in ignorance of it, as their oath stated the secret must be held perfectly or die with them.

"It was during one of these gatherings when a member of the family betrayed both their existence and their secret, for a price. The gathering and their location was tipped off and attacked by a power-hungry young sheikh, and the families and their secret were pushed into hiding in the desert while the men employed ancient skills of battle. For once in centuries, they fought in earnest, brother with father and son with son, feeling they were filling a design held from them for generations and decimating their attackers. During the skirmish, the light changed with the signs of a great storm on the horizon. They tried to end their enemies quickly so they could save their families. In a moment, they had to choose between their secret and their families, causing division among them. Each retreat of those seeking to save their families empowered their enemy. In the end, they turned and ran into the storm, desperate to find and save their loved ones.

"It was too late..." He paused. "It is said that every one of them perished in the storm. Gone. Everyone except Makar Samūm, who never left the skirmish but fought on to avenge the betrayal of his people. He still fights on, wandering the desert, searching for the remains of his family and for proof of the secret, and upholding his grisly oath that he will not stop until every man who has seen him in battle, every man who might have knowledge of their secret language of the desert, and every man responsible for the death of his great people is dead and looted and the secret they hold extinguished with them, thus fulfilling the oath that if not held perfectly, their secret must die with them."

The travelers scarcely breathed. Even the camels remained silent.

"His vengeance is insatiable, young Rashid, and all these years he has been cultivating his anger, his skill, and his lore. It's best if you fade away and live your life, remain unknown to him. That's my advice."

"That was a good one, but I believe my story is better," piped up the new traveler, unheard.

"I don't care who he thinks he is. He murdered my father…and others." Rashid looked at the Silent Tribesman and then at the fire. "For me to forget that makes him more of a legend and me more of a coward."

"Ego starts feuds, young man," Faisal replied. "Wisdom ends them. Perhaps there's more than you know. Perhaps your father saw him in that battle or knew more than you realize."

29.

The camels were notably cranky as the travelers gathered themselves to continue their journey. Rashid carried his falcon on his fist as he walked along the line of the agitated animals, admiring each one. He ran his hand along the neck of one and stopped hard. Lying across the camel was his father's red woven saddle trapping.

"This is mine," he whispered and then shouted, upsetting the falcon. He pulled it off the saddle. "This is *mine*! It was my *father's*!"

"No, it isn't," the new traveler declared, feeling affronted. "This is—"

"How do you know it's yours?" asked Faisal.

"Because I know. Because I saddled our camel every day. It was the last thing my father put on her and the first thing he removed. It has been damaged, but it's mine. Where did you get it?"

"At the market," the Silent Tribesman replied, interrupting. They looked at each other. "If you are certain it belonged to your father, then it now belongs to you."

Rashid looked at him, his face filled with fear and fury and slowly advancing realization. "First," he hissed slowly, deliberately, with seething blackness, "I will repay my debt to my uncle, and then, old man, I *will* avenge my father's death."

The Silent Tribesman sighed sadly. He turned and mounted his camel. As the stately beast rose from it's knees, his shadow fell across Rashid. "Then I'm sorry your ego will get in the way of your wisdom and your oath to your father." He leaned down and spoke slowly. "The most lost and dangerous among us are the heroes of their own stories. Should you too lose yourself in your own story and neglect the honor and life calling you, you are no different than he." He looked hard at Rashid. "Wars have been started over the very legend of such a falcon as God has given you for reasons beyond your interest to see." He sat up, his camel restless to move. "May God protect you, as your purpose will be no better than your enemy's, who today has no declaration on you."

They rode on with great effort, saying their subdued goodbyes as they scolded their unruly camels. One among them began to sing a desert ballad to soothe them while they moved as though born of the sand, following the rises into the heart of the desert. Rashid walked away from them, lost in thought, the tassels of the fingered tapestry brushing in tempo with his gait.

30.

The light of his fire pushed away the last red of twilight, and Rashid watched the stately bird rest in its warmth, lost in thought. His demeanor changed as he made a decision. He rifled through his hunting satchel and pulled out his lure. It had been shredded by the mongrel. He held it up for the dog to see, and the dog curled in guilt and profound apology. Rashid dug around for something to repair it, finding only a tasseled flag of tapestry from his father's saddle trapping and the red sash Salama had slipped into his hand. He thumbed her gift with sadness, held up the tasseled red tapestry, and looked at the falcon. "This will make you brave."

    At sunrise, Rashid began the training of the white falcon. The progression began when, after consideration, she rose from a makeshift perch to his arm, and with the troubled, tentative balance of a new partnership, she was rewarded. It culminated after many days with her joyful flight and hard stoop to his swing of the tasseled red lure with movements in a perfect dance. At last he allowed her to catch the lure, and she bound to it dutifully, taking it elegantly to ground and waiting with all her honor to trade her catch with him. With a smile, he held up his arm, draped in more red tapestry, and the falcon followed the gesture dutifully, jumping up to it in a white flurry.

    As the bird settled, a movement beyond her continued. Rashid looked to see a camel running toward him, its rider pushing him furiously with white robes flying in equal madness. He strained to see and to make sense of the scene, and among the flapping robes was the Silent Tribesman, crazily racing toward him in movement ahead of his sound. Rashid hooded the bird, crammed his things into his satchel, threw his rifle over his shoulder, and ran as fast as he could with the falcon on his arm. He sank into the sand but continued to run. The tribesman gained on him in a fury. Rashid stopped, panting, deciding. He set down the falcon and satchel, frantically loaded his rifle, shouldered it, and watched down the barrel sights as the Silent Tribesman and camel thundered at him. His finger slid to the trigger.

"Balance." He breathed. "Justice...justice." He squeezed his eyes closed.

"Get on, Rashid!"

His eyes sprang open. The tribesman was too close to be running so hard. Behind him, Rashid struggled to conceive what he was seeing. A wicked red wall of sand rose hundreds of feet, with tones too deep to hear, and moved toward them with no pity. The camel didn't stop as Rashid threw his satchel over the saddle. He paused for an instant before he handed up the white falcon.

"There are no enemies in the face of such things, Rashid. God gave her to your purpose, not mine. I swear my blood to it."

Rashid handed him the falcon, and he was barely up himself before the camel was in a full run, racing from the dark advance of the storm, the mongrel close at their heels. As they ran, Rashid could see a depression ahead, though as the storm mounted closer to them, they could feel sand being pulled from in front of them as it breathed in, gathering strength like an unfathomable predator trying to catch them. The wall curled over the top of them as they raced in the gorge of its silent giant yawn, and the camel leaped over the edge of the depression, revealing elegant stands of ribboned sandstone folding into itself.

They raced to an opening as the distance of the gape closed. The force of the thudding, blunt arrival of the storm launched them into the opening, stealing their light. Rashid looked for the mongrel, his whistle silent against the thunder and screaming of the storm. He whistled again, and the tribesman shoved him aside as he struggled to barricade the opening with the black fabric of his tent. As he pushed against the wind, Rashid helped him. When the last of the opening was closed, they heard the whisper of a plaintive bark. Rashid stepped through the cloth and was instantly swallowed into the throat of the storm. He called, and the dog bumped into him. He gathered the dog, losing his balance in the wind. He lost all sense of space but seemed to be pulled by his foot as he clutched the mongrel. The tribesman dragged him into the cave and sealed the makeshift door against the wind, plunging them into the dark.

As the storm raged, the Silent Tribesman quietly, diligently made a small fire and coffee as his camel stood stoically, like an old soul mostly unconcerned about his circumstance.

Rashid stood looking anxiously at the door, taking in the full ramification of the present moment. He was going to miss his chance to present the falcon for his uncle's dowry, and redeem himself with the sheikh. Dispirited, he sat nervously and watched the tribesman and the top of his long knife and pistol handle glint in the dim firelight, refusing the coffee offered to him.

"We may be here for some time." The tribesman continued to hold Rashid's cup.

After a long considered moment, Rashid studied the tribesman, breathed deeply, and took the coffee.

"See? Just like your falcon."

They sipped in silence, listening to the thundering of the storm. Rashid wondered whether they would be buried there like relics.

"You don't understand this, do you?" The tribesman was looking with old reverence at the white falcon. "How could you possibly understand?"

"All that matters to me is that it will make me whole in my uncle's eyes, repay my debt, and to be and worthy in the sheikh's eyes." Rashid glowered.

"So," the tribesman replied, "what you can get from her."

Rashid deflated as he sipped his coffee and politely poured them both the smallest amount more. Manners amid chaos.

"You know the reason they succeeded when the other great warriors failed was a mystery."

Rashid stared at him, confused.

"It's a mystery even now. It seemed, simply, that the desert spoke to them. More importantly, it seemed they heard it. That's why your white falcon is important. Perhaps she is the desert speaking to bring peace to your sad story; by all measures from our sands to heaven, nothing could be clearer than her presence to the broken man who killed your father. Such a bird hasn't been seen in hundreds of years."

As the tribesman talked, Rashid focused beyond the light of the fire. A blast of adrenaline pulsed through him as he spotted the corner of another tapestry, the same as his father's saddle trapping that he had rescued, tucked carefully beneath the tribesman's things. Preservation filtered into his instincts, and he fought his reaction of fear and fury behind the stillest face he could muster. His voice shook enough for the mongrel to lift his head and watch him. "This is why you saved me, isn't it? Because of some valuable white falcon you think will somehow give you a higher purpose?"

"My purpose has been spent." The tribesman's eyes dipped into memory for a breath before returning. "No, I saved you because you needed saving, didn't you? The gift of a falcon like that may only be given by God. It is the gift of protection and nobility, and it shouldn't be taken lightly, even by a sixteen-year-old boy who would give away a gift he doesn't yet understand."

"I'm seventeen."

"You won't hear me, will you?"

"Unless your stories and fantasies bring back my father...and Mohammed, no."

Rashid woke to stillness and the dim light of sharp stars. He quietly gathered his things and lifted the falcon. The starlight dimpled in the shape of their silhouette as he, the mongrel, and the falcon slipped soundlessly from the cave. The light left from the embers stirred with the fresh air and reflected in the tribesman's eyes as he watched them leave. He sighed, and his hand slid to the handle of his dagger.

Outside the entrance, Rashid felt a crack in the stone. He pulled it and it fell with a thud, blocking nearly all of the cave entrance, trapping man and camel inside.

31.

As day arrived, Rashid walked quickly through the valleys between dunes and watched behind him. He made his way to the remains of a two-track and followed it, finding a WWI truck mostly buried from the storm.

A surly, dust-covered, thirsty Englishman stood next to a tripod topped with a theodolite in similar condition, looking at the truck. They had both been shiny, elegant, and definitive of adventure and advance only months before. Now he supposed he would be spoken of reverently in hushed tones as being lost in the vastness of the empty quarter while exploring for oil. It had a nice enough ring to it, which was some small comfort, though not enough to quell his present anger. He looked up and jumped as he saw Rashid standing with a snow-white falcon on his arm and something he suspected was a dog hiding behind him. "What the hell are you?" He spat lightly, using a wayward piece of tobacco presumably as a vehicle to remove more sand. "Where are we? Hamadan? Sorud? Zabzab camp Poot etra?" He hated being there with a passion of scorn Rashid had never witnessed, and thinking all human specimens outside the British Isles would understand the only other foreign language, French, he used it with abandon. Rashid wondered if all foreigners were like this.

"Abu Dhabi."

"Abu what?" He muttered something else in French to Rashid, who didn't understand. The man had been traveling in circles.

Rashid gestured to the truck and himself.

"What! You want a ride, do you? Well, there it is. I'll make you a deal." He made pawing gestures in the sand and pointed to the submerged truck. "You dig it out, and I'll take you *anywhere* you want to go!"

Rashid flinched and looked around to see if his voice traveled, placed the falcon on a makeshift perch next to his satchel, and began to dig as the Englishman lit a well-chewed cigar.

Rashid scanned the horizon as the plumes of his efforts curtained behind him. With every movement pushing sand away, more slid into its place. He dug anyway. Through the haze left from the storm, the movement of a distant figure emerged, advancing toward them. He dug frantically, watching it gain on them while the Englishman smoked his cigar and took in the situation.

"You can dig all you want, but this pile of German garbage isn't going anywhere. Had they given me a proper British vehicle, I'd be basking on the beach at the edge of hell rather than cooking here in the middle of it." He threw the surveying equipment into the back of the truck, slid into the cab, and ground the starter. The truck sputtered and complained, and with the Englishman releasing a stream of cursing that needed no translation, it roared to life as the rider and camel crested the nearest dune. The truck's wheels spun, with Rashid pushing as the Englishman grimaced, clenching the cigar in the side of his teeth and sharing the stress of the trouble bearing down on Rashid. With a jerk, the truck found purchase, nearly stalling as it lurched forward and drove away while the camel and rider surfed down the face of the dune. After a moment, it stopped, growled painfully, and backed toward Rashid.

"Well, don't just stand there, you nitwit, or he's going to get me too! *Get in!*" the Englishman yelled.

Rashid, getting the gist of it, lifted his falcon with the only grace of the moment, threw his things in, and jumped in without upsetting a feather as the truck lumbered hard into motion. The mongrel ran with Rashid calling him, but he fell behind, disappearing in a desperate run into the dust left behind them, to Rashid's torture. He was gone. As the distance grew between them, the tribesman still chased them, continuing to yell something Rashid couldn't hear over the roar of the motor. As he fell behind, the tribesman pulled up his camel and watched as the truck lurched and bounced, disappearing into the haze of the desert.

32.

As he stepped through the subtle, curling silver vapor of oud and up from among a sea of faces, Fahad scanned with a hope imperceptible to anyone present, save for the sheikh, who watched him with measure from his niece's side. He didn't expect to see Rashid but allowed an instant for the impulse. The sadness that lingered for a moment evanesced with the sight of his bride, resplendent in the adornments of light and joy and pride in all detailed elements of tradition. He walked toward her, transfixed by her beauty and the significance of a moment he had yearned for so long. The sheikh stood beside her as Fahad approached, and with his approval, she stretched her beautiful henna-laced hand to her fiancé, and he took it. She removed a ring from his right hand and placed it on the left, and he did the same for her. Smiling, he looked up, and the gathering erupted into joyful cheers. They moved to sit next to each other in ornately adorned chairs and paused as the sound from the crowd began to change into whispers and gasps. Fahad followed the sheikh's keen focus and grinned.

"*Rashid!*"

His nephew was obscured somewhat by the crowd. Those nearest to him were wide-eyed and hushed in amazement as Rashid walked toward his uncle. He caught Saif's grin in the group and smirked knowingly. At once, Fahad's face transformed from joy to the shock of the crowd's silence as Rashid came into his full view, and his eyes began to well.

Rashid, dressed in white robes and wearing the saddle adornment over his shoulders, carried the purest white Saker falcon ever seen or considered possible by those present. They were seeing a legend. A blessing embodied. None of them could utter a word. Rashid walked up to his uncle and unhooded the great white bird, and they remained transfixed as the bird roused and looked around herself with noble comfort.

"I'm sorry to be late, Uncle. I was delayed by a storm. I hope I haven't missed it." He handed the falcon to his uncle, who struggled with his composure in the presence of such a true treasure. "Here is your dowry, Uncle."

The sheikh, also in awe, took both of their hands together and laughed in a grand, joyful boom. Fahad looked briefly at the woven saddle adornment around Rashid's shoulders and embraced him with a deeply furrowed brow. "Blessed family." He said.

With the falcon settled on a tall perch beside the wedding chairs, the ensuing ruckus and music of celebration erupted, marked by the high notes of women's trills, and settled itself joyfully over the gathering. The crowd parted as children gathered sheepishly and performed their carefully practiced dance for the bride and groom, and for their sheikh, to the drums and bells. As they finished, the crowd applauded four young ladies—draped with airy fabrics, hundreds of singing gold coins, and gold headpieces that held ten tall red lit candles—who stepped elegantly into their place and danced the Shamdan with the very movement of the flames themselves. In the midst of their magical dance, a group of ladies shrouded in gilded Bedouin silk gathered innocently in their midst. The Shamdan dancers faded into the crowd and away as the shrouded ladies fanned out to the music and stretched out their hands to the men in the gathering, the fathers and brothers of the dancers. Rashid recognized Salama as she approached the sheikh and stretched her hands toward him. Smiling, the men loosed their swords and handed them to the dancers. The music changed pace, and the women circled, handling the blades with the elegance of water, and, in perfect time and perfect orchestration, told a story belonging to them and their desert as it had since time began.

Rashid forced himself to merely glance through the glints of the blades, catching Salama's eyes before looking away. Perhaps someday she might dance at their wedding. As the music ended, Rashid realized with an embarrassed start that the sheikh was watching him. Fahad's bride whispered in his ear, and a thoughtful, measured twinkle crossed his face as he looked to Salama and back to Rashid.

"Rashid, my son, it would make me happy to have an image in my mind for old age of my beloved niece with a white falcon on her arm. Would you be so kind as to accommodate me?" He waved his niece over.

Rashid turned crimson as she approached, her face lightly obscured by aurous Bedouin silk, and walked her to the falcon, handing her the ornate cuff. She settled her hand and arm into it, and he guided it to the falcon, holding the leash for her. The great white bird stepped gallantly to the cuff. Salama studied the hood, and seeing the pearl and red plume, her expression changed in recognition and understanding. She glanced at Rashid with the hint of a knowing smile, and he reached to the hood, loosened the braces, and removed it from the bird's head. The falcon, inexplicably comfortable in her surroundings, fluffed her feathers and roused. She turned and looked directly at Salama and then to the gathering and to Rashid. When she saw Rashid, she dipped her head and playfully tilted it upside down. Salama laughed, to Rashid's silent joy.

He looked down. "She will speak to you. Like all things, if you respect her and listen to her instead of yourself, she will show you all ways and will die for you if she must."

Salama looked at him in astonishment as he spoke.

"Pull on her mouth and you'll have to answer to me." He looked for a smile and received none.

"Rashid this is your falcon, not your uncle's. Like Malaak chose me, she chose you."

The magic of the evening sustained itself with shadowless joy. Rashid allowed the relief to wash over him for a while as one would with cool water during a hard walk through the desert. He watched the sheikh admiring the falcon as Fahad held her on his arm. Fahad smiled at him, and Rashid saw his father's face in the expression. He sighed, knowing his journey was not yet done.

"May I speak with you, Your Highness?" Rashid asked.

"Of course, young falconer." The three of them walked into the garden. "Before you speak, Rashid"—the sheikh locked gazes with him as he spoke—"you need to know that your uncle has given me reason to doubt your story about the circumstances surrounding Mohammed's death." He held Rashid's gaze with a careful depth of reason and gave a nearly imperceptible wink.

Rashid glanced at his uncle, then back to the sheikh, who spoke with animated pronouncement.

"He then noted to me that Mohammed suffered a gunshot wound. He also noticed that Malaak had blood down his shoulder. Now, I ask myself, why would a man go through all of that trouble to rescue someone he himself shot...with a firearm he did not have?" Rashid nodded, understanding that he needed to take the sheikh's lead.

"Thank you, uncle." Rashid said carefully.

Fahad handed the falcon back to Rashid, looking at her with longing. "God did not send her to you to be wasted rectifying yourself to me. Especially as you are innocent." As he transferred the seraphic bird to his nephew, he clapped Rashid's shoulder and looked closely at the tapestry there.

"It was my father's..." Rashid looked hard at Fahad, who continued to thumb and study the textile, falling for an instant into memory.

"Blessed family," Fahad said quietly with more nostalgia than he had before.

"Makar Samūm killed Mohammed," Rashid said to the sheikh.

"You've seen him?" asked the sheikh.

Rashid nodded gravely.

Fahad breathed a deep, saddened sigh.

"He knows who I am. So either I must die, or he must." Rashid said, feeling the weight of it as he said it out loud for the first time.

"You're determined to kill him?" asked the sheikh.

Rashid nodded.

"Because of protection or to avenge your father?"

Rashid couldn't answer.

"It's an answer you need to find within yourself. As it goes against the final wishes of your father to kill this man, without that answer, it puts me in a difficult position. Without certainty, I cannot protect you."

Fahad looked sadly at Rashid, as though saying goodbye. "Rashid, are you certain of this?" He saw the answer on his nephew's face. "Each man's justice is his own...As it was against my brother's wishes for it to come to this, I must protest, though I understand it. I don't want to lose my family."

"How will you find him?" asked the sheikh.

"He knows where he murdered my father."

The sheikh's guard who had escorted Rashid into the falcon tent walked to the sheikh and whispered something to him. He looked at the guard with surprise.

"Hold a wedding and everyone shows up. I must go receive this guest. Rashid, take Saif's camel. He has become mostly yours as it is. He'll get you there quickly, and you'll be obliged to return him to Saif yourself." He patted Rashid on the shoulder. "I would bid that God be with you, but it would seem He already is."

Rashid walked from the glow into the light of the full wedding moon.

33.

The thought of sunrise etched the silhouette of the threesome into sharp and proper continuation of the line of a dune. Timeless in like fashion, the desert was surely pleased at its artistry as it gave the day a horizon that reminded it how many millions they had shared together through the ages. As if to answer the pleasure of God in that moment, Rashid unhooded his falcon, cast her off for Him, and watched the beautiful arc of her flight carry her higher than he could see. He pulled out the red lure and swung it into the breath of the oncoming day, and she appeared from heaven in a joyful stoop, knocking it to the ground, binding to it, and winning the game. He raised his hand with a whistle, and she flew to it, accepting the tidbit of shrike he held for her. He wound the line, pulled in the lure as she ate, and noticed something about the design in the tapestry. He grabbed the tapestry draped over his saddle and looked closely at it. Woven subtly into the reds were tiny white flecks. He turned the piece around and studied them. His eyes widened in disbelief. The flecks were each the shape of a perfect white falcon in flight. Thousands of them.

    He looked at his bird, rousing and feaking the shrike blood from her beak. She looked at him and playfully tipped her head. Her attention pulled to the desert, and her demeanor changed. Her easy stance shifted to predator, and she bobbed her head, a falcon's gesture warning that she had found her prey. Rashid followed her gaze and pulled up his camel.

His adrenaline surged as they walked silently around a dune, the place Rashid's father had died appearing in the distance. They stopped. Anger and pain washed over him, accompanied by a nervous anchor of fear. The lone gnarled little tree and mound of stones were kept company by a lone seated figure facing away from him. Adrenaline pumped through Rashid, sharpening and shaping everything. He backed up, removed his rifle from its place behind him, placed the falcon on the fork of the saddle, and dropped noiselessly to the ground. He slid as though part of the desert toward the tree, leaned over the top of a small rise, steadied his rifle, and breathed. For an eternity it seemed, both he and the figure remained motionless.

"Justice. Balance…" He breathed, curling the trigger in his finger. "Respect." As though the figure knew he had spoken, it stood and disappeared into the depression where Rashid and his father had camped. Rashid ran low toward the tree, then dropped and squinted down his rifle waiting.

The heat of the young day drew silver lines through the image appearing where the figure had disappeared. Rashid's breath caught in his chest. First the saddle carrying all his father's belongings appeared from the mercury, followed by the face and legs of his beloved Al Rabea. Beside her, the silver waves gave way to the form of a dark-red ghutrah atop a head.

The falcon's head bobbed deeply as she shifted hard into yarak. Rashid shared her focus, squared the wavy figure in his sights, and waited to see him through the heat waves that moved the image of him swaying and collecting into form. "Justice." His finger moved against the trigger.

The face of the figure formed and focused from the silver, the blood-red fabric curling and billowing like a flag around it.

"The thing that cannot be undone," his father's voice whispered from the desert.

The face beneath the swaying red cleared into focus. Fahad looked directly at him with clarity and acknowledgment. Rashid stood up, looking at him. Fahad bent down, picked up a handful of desert, raised his hand, and unfurled a veil as the sand fell toward the ground and was taken on the breeze. Neither of them moved as it ran slowly from his hand. Fahad turned and sat next to his brother's grave, his hand on a lower stone. Rashid picked up his rifle and walked toward his uncle, heart pounding with anger, betrayal, and sadness.

"Take your hand off of that stone." Rashid spat.

"We have always had falcons. Did he not tell you? That is our secret. Falcons told us where the game was, where our enemies were, and how they advanced."

Rashid didn't move.

"I never could figure out how. They never taught me how." His expression changed to that of a little boy rejected by his brothers.

"Our name comes from a lost language; it means People of the Longwing." Fahad looked painfully at the grave as he explained the secret of the falcon people. "Once every generation, God gave them to us. But not to mine. Your falcon is the first white bird to appear for us in hundreds of years. The best of our ancestors, they're all in her. All my life, the Saker eluded me. I always thought someday I might trap the one that proved my nobility, but God sent her to you."

"What nobility, Fahad?"

"We were royalty, Rashid. We were revered much, much more even than our sheikh. And we had the skill to protect it. We were called to the reaches of our world for our help. We fought off the Turks and Alexander the Great by our prowess, but instead of using it to create a great society, our ancestors were cowards and hid from it, living like rats in the desert. Hiding from what we are.

"I had it restored...He was going to give it *all* to us. Our own kingdom at last, as we have so long deserved, and the recognition that is our right. We were the guests and favored by Sheikh Morad himself, a powerful ally." He spoke the name with a hungry reverence. "To make us whole and to join his family, he merely asked for the secret from of how the desert spoke to them, but my father laughed out loud in his face and said he had never heard of such a thing. He betrayed me knowing it would cost my life. I told them somehow it was the falcons. Your father laughed with him at the ridiculousness of such a notion. 'They're for catching our suppers and some sport, nothing more,' your grandfather told them. They made a fool of me. And a liar." He blackened. "My blood...they betrayed me." He continued, growing angrier.

"Sheikh Morad. He held his knife to my father and demanded the secret of our people from your father..." Fahad faded into a memory of his father with a curved knife across his neck, looking at him sadly and then saying to his brother beside him, "Remember your oath."

"Your father, my brother, stood there stupidly and refused even then, calling me a fool and we a people of common peasants with one ignorant power-hungry brother." Fahad grew wide-eyed at the memory. "And he killed him...Even as our father lay dying, my brothers present maintained it and never told it. The cowards could have saved him by telling but allowed him to die that way. In disgrace. Sheikh Morad leaned in and whispered something to him, and your father killed Sheikh Morad, our last ally, to spite me and end my chances, and a battle ensued. Another brother, the eldest and my protector, Marwan, was killed, but our legend was proven by our fierceness in battle, until a wind approached and my brothers and uncles turned and ran like cowards. I stayed to prove our legend, but I was the only one. They all perished in that storm, except your father...and you.

"I have lived two lives, Rashid. One to build myself into the position of nobility that is our birthright. Another to eradicate any existence of that story or anyone who would connect me to it. There is no legend, no secret, and no family. There is only the future I am building."

"Including murdering my father."

"Especially your father. He was going to be my crown jewel. My last one. I gave him the chance to save himself. All he had to do was tell me the secret to prove it existed. He refused." Fahad breathed deeply. "The oath remains that the secret must be held perfectly or die with us. So it died with your Father." He looked at Rashid, grew distant and turned to the grave. "But...I didn't anticipate you, Rashid. Had I known my brother had a son, I may not have killed him. You are an innocent." He looked away. "I trained you, certain you would tip your hand and reveal what he taught you. I saw that your father died with our secret to protect you. It gave me some measure of peace knowing there was nothing more than to live in what nobility I had earned for myself. I saw your skill and hoped we could build our family empire back, together."

"And Mohammed?" asked Rashid. "Why him?"

"I couldn't risk him. Mohammed was a casualty of getting too close. He sold your father's camel trappings and heard too much. He had seen Al Rabea and was a breath from knowing everything." He shook his head. "And he was jealous of you."

"What now? I know your story," said Rashid carefully.

"And you know yours," replied Fahad. "You now have a choice to make. Are you a man of the desert after all? Are you a man who will honor your family and build on its new legacy with me? I've already done the hard work."

"Would God have given a white falcon to a person who was willing to protect a murderer, Fahad?"

"That falcon is a symbol of our family, of our nobility! Don't you understand? Doesn't her appearance now tell you this is justified, Rashid?"

"No. That falcon is a sign of our ancestors' dedication to the protection of the just and the nobility of balance. Protecting our ancestors doesn't mean avenging something in our imagination."

"With your new heritage as a noble, you can ask to marry Salama. Without it, you're just another common desert rat who doesn't stand a chance. Don't you want that?"

"So I could dishonor her by asking her to be a sellout with me?" He turned away to hide the jab through his heart for her. "You have fooled yourself to think that you're on some crusade, so you exploited the story, our story, *my* story, to justify your own personal greed for a meaningless glory, and you have illustrated the reason my grandfather and my father and uncles protected it from you! Even in death, they protected our history. You"—Rashid snorted—"you're nothing but a common thug murderer." He rounded on Fahad. "And knowledge or not, you took my father from me, you murdered Mohammed, and you destroyed my past and a gift my family protected and used rightly for more than a thousand years...all destroyed for yourself."

"Then kill me. It's a respectable and just answer, Rashid."

"To you, perhaps. But it will be much better to kill your story and leave you with what you have already earned: shame and obscurity."

Rashid untied Al Rabea and walked away from his uncle. Fahad called him as he walked away, tearing off his scarlet ghutrah and shaking it at Rashid.

"Do you know what this is? It's respect! It's our family!"

"It's cloth. An empty myth you have borrowed and exploited. A lie," replied Rashid over his shoulder. "Soon to be righted for my father. For balance. For justice."

Fahad's anger tipped to desperation and fury, revealing a glimpse of the searing, crazed detachment of the murderer. He pushed the red ghutrah crazily on his head, picked up his rifle, and lifted it to his shoulder with Rashid in view.

"*Rashid!*" He watched down the barrel to see his nephew turn to face the rifle. As his finger found the trigger, a desert breeze pushed the red silk snaking across his face. Rashid didn't move. Above him, the white falcon streaked from the clouds, fixed hard on the red ghutrah, the same deep crimson as her lure. Fahad's finger squeezed the trigger.

34.

The speed of bullets and falcons are reverently compared out of honor to the spirit of the living thing. From before bronze and antiquity, it was the honored bullet of man. One with a soul and decision belonging more to God and less to the obstructions of man. It is by God that her speed is given and proven superior to the things of men when He wills it.

Perhaps it was thus that in that otherwise still moment, the bullet traveled the barrel, and the great white falcon struck the red ghutrah, knocking it and its contents forward with a force of speed given by something beyond human understanding, tipping man and rifle to the ground as the bullet exited and his head hit the carved gun stock. Fahad crumpled, dropping the rifle. He raised his head, struggling to make sense of his surroundings and what had happened to him as the red flagged around his face. She struck him again, and he found himself on his side, forcing himself into consciousness, seeing through the sideways haze the white falcon turning on her wing to come back for her killing strike. He righted himself and, with the clarified effort of pure preservation, chambered a bullet and raised his rifle to her. As she streaked toward him and he struggled to steady his aim, his thought split, and he lowered the rifle to Rashid. Finger to trigger, he blinked. A shot echoed.

Fahad's eyes rose from Rashid and widened as they focused behind him. The falcon struck and missed. He was already falling. Rashid whirled around to see the Silent Tribesman with his rifle still shouldered, watching Fahad fall, crumpling on the pile of rocks over his brother's grave. The sheikh stood beside his camel behind the tribesman, with the mongrel at his side and Mohammed standing behind him.

The tribesman dismounted, ran to Fahad, and dropped in anguish to the dying man. Rashid followed him. Fahad raised his blood-covered hand and stared at it with a calm shock of inevitability. He looked up from his hand at the figure causing this shade surrounding him.

"Marwan?" he whispered, wondering for a moment which world he occupied.

"Brother," rumbled the tribesman quietly.

Fahad's face screwed into the emotional grimace releasing a lifetime of pain. "You were dead. Where have you been?" murmured Fahad.

"I have been living in death with my truth, looking for you, little brother, to explain our story, while hiding from Makar Samūm, who wouldn't have heard it. Father and Majid didn't betray you. They protected you by not telling you. You're alive now because of them."

"You don't know. They abandoned me. They didn't stand behind me. They made a fool of me and what I had built for us."

"I was there, little brother. Had you known our secret, the gift of the desert, we, your brothers, would have had to kill you by the oath we took. Father stepped in front of Sheikh Morad as he was about to use you to force the secret. By not telling you, he protected you from the sheikh and from all of us who loved you. He died protecting you. I was the one who killed Sheikh Morad. I am the one carrying the blood-vengeance price. Me. Not you. In the skirmish, Majid found me and tried to help me as the storm came. I sent him into the storm, forcing him to leave me for dead. We left you there fighting so we could save the falcons, which we did...and our families, which we did not. They returned for you but found only death."

Rashid looked up and raised his hand. The falcon rose to it, and in a white flurry, she landed. He clipped to her jesses.

"It's them, isn't it? The falcons. They're it, somehow, aren't they? Please, brother. Tell me."

Marwan leaned down and spoke low to his brother, in an old voice belonging to generations before them. "We are the People of the Longwing. We are the noble protectors..." He spoke to his brother for a long time, until Fahad sighed in relief and peace and smiled.

"What does it say that I was killed by our protector?" he said with the lingering air in his lungs, staring at the great white Saker.

"It means you have died a noble death and you can be at peace," said his brother. "They have come back to us to speak."

"Rashid. You can hear her. But you already knew that, didn't you? That is our secret. Marwan will teach you... keep it perfectly and make it live another thousand years." Fahad winced in pain, feeling his life retreat. "First," he whispered with nearly no breath left in him, "remember what we do for falcons that have been good to us." Rashid nodded, and Fahad touched the falcon's breast, leaving blood on her white feathers. He smiled weakly at the red and white and passed out of this life in that very place where Rashid had watched his father go.

Rashid stood and looked at the sheikh before walking away from the scene. With tears rolling down his handsome cheeks and beard, he stood in the evening sun, removed the hood and jesses from the great white Saker falcon, fed her the last of the shrike, and touched the drying blood on her feathers, noticing it was remarkably in the shape of a falcon. She held fast to time as she looked into him, anchoring his growing certainty of who he was. She tipped her head playfully and roused her feathers with elegance and comedy, and he softly cast her into flight. The three men stood in the silence of the desert's evening embrace and watched her rise.

The sheikh placed his hand over Rashid's shoulder like a father and slowly spoke to his sadness. "You have brought an uncle out of a death he didn't deserve and brought another to a death he did deserve with a grace befitting your people. You did all of it while not betraying your father. You have restored honor back to your noble family. You have justice. And, young man, you have my respect."

"Thank you, Highness, but that won't help me ask you what I…"

"That's true," replied the sheikh. "Those aren't very right terms, are they?" The sheikh turned to look at Rashid. "I think perhaps God is still speaking."

Rashid looked at him.

"You know…the only person who knew Mohammed was not dead was Salama."

Rashid looked at him. "You sent her?"

"She sent herself." The sheikh shook his head in mock desperation. "I should have listened to her. I thought her protests about her cousin marrying Fahad were simple bouts of jealousy, and her disdain for him innocent protectiveness." He shook his head. "We had no other way to protect Mohammed from Makar Samūm than to declare him dead, and I hadn't decided how to address punishing you to hold up the story." Rashid looked straight at him and the great sheikh returned the gaze, shaking his head slowly with a sideways smile waiting to see if Rashid would figure out the rest.

"Salama ransacked the falcons, didn't she?" Rashid said with detached amazement. "So it would create a diversion..."

"And it would push you away from your uncle." The sheikh's eyes twinkled. "Quite ingenious, actually. She gave you no other choice. You must have done something right with her horse, because it seems that she likes you."

With the full picture of Salama's thinking that evening settling on him, Rashid thought. "I'll replace the falcons for you, Highness. With Mohammed's help. I'll pay her debt."

"Did I never mention that Salama is the daughter of my murderous brother, Sheikh Morad?"

Rashid looked hard at him, knitting together the significance of what he had said.

"If I'm not mistaken, he owed you quite a debt." The sheikh's eyes twinkled. "And as you know, if we become related in time, there's nothing like family to protect their secrets, and each other..."

The amazed smile that broke across Rashid's face despite his best efforts was one of a man having survived a storm.

"Yes, my dear boy. There is a bright lore yet to be spun. The legend of Desert Falcon, the descendent of mythical warriors who bested the great Makar Samūm with the secret of his ancestors. A far fresher and nobler hero, wouldn't you say?"

The Silent Tribesman—Rashid's uncle, Marwan—joined the sheikh and his nephew. They watched the white falcon tilt on her wing and rocket around them, lifting their joy with hers. Then, tilting her wings in a farewell to them, their noble protector lifted and joined the gold clouds on the horizon. As Marwan watched, coming more to life with each beat of her wings, he looked at his nephew and laughed deeply for the first time in seventeen years.

35.

"Coffee? Pardon, sir, but would you like some coffee? We'll be landing soon." The flight attendant was gentle and apologetic but wanted to check on her favorite passenger.

The old man woke painfully, gathered his faculties, and smiled at her.

"I'll get some for you." She winked. "The sunrise is beautiful out there. You should raise your shade and enjoy it."

His curled, knobby fingers worked to open the shade, and he squinted at the brilliance of it. He looked, as he always had, for a white falcon soaring among the clouds.

As he walked through the gate and across the floors of the Abu Dhabi airport, children of different generations rushed to him. He feigned a grouchy response but smiled at them all and looked down as the delicate little hand of his great-granddaughter slipped into his own. He leaned slowly down and whispered just to her, to her utter joy, "You are lovelier. Where is Sittu?"

She smiled and pointed, as if part of giving a present. He looked up to see her, and his wrinkled, tired face was consumed by affection. All the children smiled. They knew what was coming.

"How is it, my beloved, that you become more beautiful each time I see you?" The sweet elderly Salama stood with the careful guard of a handsome sixteen-year-old boy at her elbow.

Though strong and storied, her face blushed, and she smiled. As they waited for his luggage, Salama whispered to him, "Are you sure this isn't too much for a young boy?"

Rashid patted her hand. "It's perfectly right, beloved." He smiled at her with satisfaction and called his great-grandson. "Fahad, come with me. I need your hands."

They moved slowly to the luggage desk, where a well-dressed guard waited politely for Rashid's shaky hands to retrieve a folded stack of papers from an elegant carry-on, slowly unfold them, and present them. The guard looked at the papers and then back up to Rashid, his expression quietly holding more respect than before.

"We've been waiting for this. I'll be right back."

A tough Range Rover rolled through the desert as the distant, jagged towers of the shimmering city faded below the horizon of dunes. It passed a black wool Bedouin tent with a few handsome, smiling men emerging to watch them drive by.

"Father. Uncle..." the boy said in confusion.

"Keep driving," fussed Rashid. The truck stopped at a lone ancient, gnarled tree that boasted only a few leaves. Rashid stiffly, gingerly stepped from the car and walked to the two mounds of stones beneath it. He reached down and patted the stones, then turned to his great-grandson.

"As you have proven your integrity to your father, your uncles, and to me, I have something very important to tell you. A truth of your family that stretches far before Alexander the Great, that saved great cities and civilizations like Petra, and that helped great Bedouin tribes. In the tradition of the noble people that were your ancestors, you must give your solemn promise, as they gave theirs, to be made on the very lives of those whom you love the most and whom you will love, that what I'm about to share will never be told to anyone but your sons and daughters, who also give their promise to its secrecy."

Young Fahad was a little shaken by the seriousness of this normally gentle, wise man. "I promise, Grandfather. I promise I won't say a word."

Rashid walked to the back of the truck and opened the door, revealing a white box with a latch and airline stickers, then reached in with quiet, schooled movement. The boy caught his breath as Rashid emerged wearing a crimson ghutrah and with a very pale Saker falcon on his left hand and a long, worn red tapestry in the other. He placed the falcon on the arm of the lad.

"We are the People of the Longwing…We are the noble protectors…" Behind them rose a great white Saker falcon. As she flew joyfully higher through another history, she could see that behind Rashid, young Fahad, and their new falcon, there weren't two graves of brothers of the longwing, but all three together. She rose higher to see the tents and the men wearing red walking in kinship to their newest son and brother as they had for thousands of years. She rose higher, tipping her wings to their ancient story as the shining metropolis of their future rose from against the sea before her, and in her wings, she gathered together their past and their future once again. The sound of wind and sand whispered together as she, a single pale falcon, passed through an impossibly blue sky. Those who would see her or know she was there were forever under the spell of her freedom as she rose higher. Higher.

Then she sublimated slowly, as if into the robes of her desert grandmother and the legend of our imagination.

Desert Falcon

Printed in Poland
by Amazon Fulfillment
Poland Sp. z o.o., Wrocław